Anna Goeldin – The Last Witch
A Novel

Anna Goeldin -
The Last Witch
A Novel

Eveline Hasler

**Translation from the German
by Mary Bryant**

**Edited with Historical Background by
Waltraud Maierhofer**

Anna Goeldin - The Last Witch. A Novel

© Eveline Hasler 2018, English translation Mary Bryant 2018

Published in Switzerland and Germany as *Anna Göldin – Letzte Hexe.
Roman* by Benziger Verlag, Zürich and Köln, 1982.

This book is a work of fiction. Named locations are used fictitiously, and characters and incidents are the product of the author's imagination. See the "afterword" and "Historical Background" about the actual case behind it. Anna Goeldi was rehabilitated in 2008.

All rights reserved. Without limiting the rights under copyright reserved above, no part of this publication may be reproduced, stored in a retrieval system, or transmitted, in any form or by any means (electronic, mechanical, photocopying, recording or otherwise), without the prior written permission of the copyright owner of this book.

Published by
Lighthouse Christian Publishing
SAN 257-4330
5531 Dufferin Drive
Savage, Minnesota, 55378
United States of America

www.lighthousechristianpublishing.com

Contents

Passages in italics have been adapted from the extant trial documents or other documents as listed in the acknowledgments.

"And when the tempter came to him, he said, If thou be the Son of God, command that these stones be made bread."

(Matthew 4:3)

1

Anna of sad renown.

Stones wherever you look, going back on her trail. In Sennwald, where Göldin grew up, there are steeply sloping meadows and fields full of boulders. Bluffs extend out of them, mountains with jagged edges, horns, crumbling rocks.

At some point in time, there was a rockslide down the Kreuzberg into the Rhine; fir trees near Salez grasp boulders with their roots. Nothing is rolling nowadays, the dust has settled. Birds fly among the branches, a sanctimonious peace.

Stones even gave the small barony its names: *sax, sassum* — stone. In 1615, when the barons of Sax ran out of money and only stones were left over, they sold the region to Zurich; it would remain under the "authority and dominion of the honorable estate of Zurich" until the revolution.

The people of Zurich, who had paid for their freedom with their lives and possessions, sent governors, now Ziegler, now Ulrich, to live at castle Forstegg on the bluffs of the mountain precipice where the beech trees parted to form a clearing. He sat at his heavy oak table, keeping neat accounts of his subjects in books labeled "Free" and "Bound." Both free and bound families were listed there, as well as those in which the categories of subservience were blended: if a free woman married a serf or vice versa, then the first child belonged to the governor, the second was free, the third belonged to the governor, and so on. But even the so-called "freemen" were subject to the authority of Zurich; they bought their freedom from only certain duties. Following Anna's trail, I searched these books for records of the stony fields' farmers. As early as the 18th Century, more than a third of the inhabitants of Sennwald were named Göldi. A name that housed little gold, but one for which dialect dictionaries indicated the root words *gôl* and *gôleten* — boulders and gravel. The first names were similar, too: as many Anna Göldins as there were Annas.

At the time when Anna was born, at the end of August 1734, her father had planted his first potatoes and a stretch of corn they called "Turks." These new plants allowed them to avoid the governmental tithes for a while. Approbated and authorized by the noble lords of Zurich, the bylaws limped behind. This reprieve allowed the people to survive.

There was a massive boulder in Adrian Göldi's flax field. The child Anna knew it well, its cracks, its notches where quaking grass and wild geraniums grew, its pale veins of quartz. A castle with crenellations, a miniature Forstegg in the field of flax. The goats on the stone raised their horns up to the windy skies streaked with stringy clouds. Anna and her sister Barbara climbed up after them and chased them off with hazel braches.

The governor did not like the stone.

He was certain the fields would be more productive if they were cleared. He sent a servant from the castle to help Anna's father blow up the boulder.

Her mother watched from the doorway with the children hanging on her skirt, curiosity and fear in their faces. No! No! Anna cried, but the men did not listen. They turned their backs and busied themselves with powder and fuse.

The boulder spat out stones as big as a fist. They drummed down on the flax field and rumbled through the young corn.

One should not tamper with the stones, Father's father had said. He's tampered with everything, they said over and over about the governor, because he's a bully, he's a belligerent warhorse.

They wanted to get rid of one stone, but now it had given birth to hundreds. They were in the soil, they filled the cornfields whispering in the wind. The children bent down, gathered them up, and felt their aching backs.

2

In September 1780, Anna took her final position in the home of Herr Tschudi, doctor and judge of the Court of Five in Glarus.

She has already been in Glarnerland once, then moved away, and then came back again, changing employment numerous times, weaving an intricate trail.

First here, then there.

And this at an age in life when others would have long held a steady position. No other woman does this sort of thing.

At least not one of her status.

Disregarding the law of stones, which lie where they fall. Her relatives say she should have stayed in Sennwald. One stays where one belongs. Anyone who doesn't stay belongs nowhere.

Her own fault.

A little over forty years old, and still this desire to change. To search for a different corner, another place under a strange roof, at another hearth.

She pulls at the bell-rope and looks up at the wall, her head tipped back against her neck. One of those old-fashioned mansions typical of Glarnerland: five levels, steep gables, a little tower over the stairwell. Massive and defiant, a small castle. The houses have to be immense if they hope to endure between the mountain walls.

She would have liked to serve in one of the mansions built in the newest styles, with round gables, columned facades, gardens with miniature flower beds and labyrinths, for example at the house "in the meadow," where Blumer, the factory owner, is living now. But even the house standing before her is worth it. It is a matter of professional honor, when one has taken each step on one's career as a servant, to have letters of recommendation to show from the best houses. At fourteen she began as a farm maid in Meyenfeldt, in a farmyard where the rooms were small and dirty and there was hardly any more to eat than at her parents' home, which she'd had to leave so as not to starve.

It was much more comfortable at the gunsmith's in Sax, or she wouldn't have stayed for six years, but in comparison to the manse in Sennwald, she'd had only to do simple housekeeping. She was envied for her position at the manse. The others were naïve — she'd been naïve herself — to consider the rustic wooden house genteel. She learned what genteel truly was when she came to Glarnerland, to the Zwicki family's home in Mollis. Certainly the Zwicki house, a position for an entire life, was a dream come true for any maid once she had beaten ideas of marriage out of her head. A comfortable house, food in plenty, kind employers. But it had not become a position for life; life caught up with her, it shook her up and drove her away. Establish yourself. Once and for all. She hasn't managed to yet. Wherever she goes, waves ripple, as if a stone has been thrown in.

The Tschudi family will be her eighth or ninth employer, if she doesn't count her positions in between, with the master of the fishery in St. Gallen and the bookbinder in Glarus. In the event that it works out with this position.

But she has no doubts about that. It is apparent on a maid's face if she understands something of economy. Anyone who is equipped with insight into human nature can see it. Anyone who does not see it doesn't deserve a good maid.

Her hand skims along the door latch, dark yellow brass, almost tarnished, and the metal hinges are not polished either. When she is in charge of the house, it will shine!

And the sandstone steps are dirty; scratches from cleaning are visible. One of those ignorant young maids has been at work there, scrubbing it with a tuff stone, a farmer's tool. She herself had used such outdated methods at the pastor's in Sennwald. Then, in the Zwicki house she had been educated on this. Footsteps are approaching now. She adjusts her bonnet and straightens her Sunday dress.

An old woman leads her to the staircase. Anna inhales the sharp scent of medicines, the fragrances of home, of the Zwicki house, of the medical practice Melchior opened on the first floor after his father died.

The living room is spacious and brightly lit, but Anna is surprised. Although it is a clear day outside the windows are dark, filled with the imposing cliffs nearby. The ceiling is decorated with stucco ornamentation: allegories of the seasons. The sofa, the curved chairs with flowery patterns, a wall-sized mirror framed in gold, a tiled stove with a dome and country scenes on the tiles. A buffet with pewter pitchers, silver medals of honor.

She is pleased as she swiftly takes stock of the room with a practiced eye that is always busy in strangers' homes. She does not let herself get too comfortable. She has her pride.

Employers do not suspect that their houses really belong to their maids and cats.

Relationships are weaved among the walls and furniture. They would look like spider webs if they were visible. The lady of the house sitting at the back of the room next to the window puts down her embroidery, colorful threads and needles, and approaches the maid.

Hello, Frau Doctor, I am Anna Göldin.

Steinmüller the locksmith, who told her this morning about the vacant position, knows that Elsbeth Tschudi is in her late twenties and has five children; he's distantly related to her. He praised her facial features and her skin: white, as fine and transparent as an English teacup when you hold it to the light.

Odd comparison. Anna must not laugh. The pinched lines around her mouth, the tiny wrinkles above her brows; have they escaped his twinkling eyes, damaged by his work at the forge?

Of course, on days when the dry föhn wind blows down from the mountains, the light is like a knife blade. Its keen edge mercilessly exposes every imperfection.

Now the master of the house comes into the parlor, too, just dropping in to see who has been admitted into the house.

Hello, Herr Doctor and Judge.

She is familiar with the multitude of titles in Glarus, a bundle of peacock feathers brought back from military service in foreign parts, inherited, purchased, and raffled off. Everyone to whom these things matter sticks as many as possible into his hat: Herr Lieutenant, Commandant, Morals Court Judge, Judge of the Court of Five or Court of Nine, Counselor, Baronet, Treasurer… Later, when the talk of evil deeds is going around, they will say that she "was not an inept individual" in societal matters.

A stately figure of a woman, thinks Doctor Tschudi, not a pale creature like the last one, who had twigs for arms and could hardly be expected to carry a water jug. She's not quite young anymore. Yet nor does she show any signs of old age.

How old are you?

About forty.

Discretion for the years that have gathered about her like weeds. A private matter. She knows that people guess her to be younger; under her bonnet her curly hair is dark, without the blending of gray. Those who must constantly shake the dust from their feet remain young. He who sits still grows stiff. She is any boy's match in energy and mobility.

The doctor has recently engrossed himself in Lavater's *Physiognomic Fragments*: she is of full but well-proportioned stature, her neck is flexible, her quick gray eyes attest to a bright mind. Her strong nose, narrow at the bridge, speaks of independence, and her chin, too, expresses autonomy, while the down-slanting oval face promises harmony and balance.

Healthy, without a doubt.

It is evident in her bright, clear skin and the rosy spots below her temples, which indicate good digestion and blood flow.

A reliable, proper individual.

Better than an unripened creature like Stini, their last maid. He has just read an alarming essay by his colleague Friedrich Benjamin Osiander on the penchant of young maids for arson. Passion for fire or an addiction to setting things alight is related to the hematological situation of women. During developmental years, the female sex is ruled by overpowering venosity; venous congestion around the optical nerves produces avarice for light… Theories, examples of which have been documented even here in Glarnerland. Recently a sixteen-year-old girl in Näfels, without any history of conflict, set fire to her employers' home…

So it is important to look closely at one's servants.

We can expect something from this maid, thinks Frau Tschudi. She is experienced and adept at all sorts of housework, so she can be left to be independent and have free reign.

But just such a thing is a horrid thought.

And her body takes up twice as much room as Frau Tschudi's does.

Of course, she has had such bad luck with the young ones such as Stini, too passive and timid. She let the children walk all over her, then finally it was too much, and yesterday she up and left. At a time like this, when guests are invited to dinner. It would be just too unseemly to send away Lieutenant Becker, former Canton President Heer, and Baronet Zwicki; it would run through town like wildfire. People are already talking about their inability to keep a serving maid for any length of time. This one here appears as if she could easily eat twelve people's meals and be ready for more only a short while later…

Nevertheless. She is not sure.

Maybe it has to do with the demeanor of this Göldin; there is nothing submissive about her. She has known others who wrung their hands, pleading for employment. This one stands tall, candidly returning her gaze.

It occurs to her that this woman's clothing is much too proud. Frau Tschudi examines Göldin's dress. A skirt in the current fashion! Only Frau Lieutenant Marti wears a skirt like that; shimmery violet interwoven with brown is supposedly the latest fashion in Paris. At their last Tea Society meeting, the women agreed that nowadays they had to take a second glance to distinguish between the upper class and the servants.

And the silk ribbon around her neck, what a silly fashion. The peasants call it a "Bettli" and supposedly it makes the skin of the throat appear whiter.

Anna meets her scrutinizing look.

Where have you been employed? The woman asks quickly.

A few places. With the master of the fishery in St. Gallen, then in Sennwald at a manse…

And in Glarnerland? The doctor wants to know.

Most recently with a bookbinder. Before that at another manse.

Where?

In Mollis.

She senses his thoughtful gaze, blushes, and flounders as she explains that the pastor died during her fourth year of service there, and then she remained with the pastor's wife and their grown children, one of them became a doctor…

Is that the Zwickis who live on Kreuzgasse?

Yes, them.

How strange, thinks Dr. Tschudi, that she counts the Zwickis among her less remarkable employers! Good grief and no end, this is something to be proud of! Served the Zwicki-Zwicki family, the richest in the country, or so people say, in a grand house, with a mistress renowned for her charity and hospitality! A reference for anyone who served in that house. And she mentions her employment there so offhandedly. But were they happy with her when she left?

Do you have a reference from the Zwickis?

She takes a piece of paper from her handbag and hands it to him.

An employment reference, signed by Dorothea Zwicki-Zwicki, widow to Johann Heinrich, former pastor in Bilten, now resting in the Lord. She warmly recommends the maid. She regrets her sudden departure and gives her blessings for her continued journey.

What was acceptable to the Zwickis is good enough for him. Particularly with the prospect that she has learned a delectable cuisine in the hospitable home. They can expect her to be a good cook from the look of her: plump, red-cheeked, clean, vitality in her face.

Did you cook at the Zwicki house?

To satisfaction, if I may say so.

She is sparing with words. None of the usual torrent of affected speeches, oaths, assurances, as he is used to from women hoping to gain favor.

It is fine with me if Anna Göldin remains with us. Why delay? I have to get back to my work in the office.

The Frau Doctor remarks that perhaps she might have a say in the decision?

His smile curdles. I thought we were pressed for… The chickens are already being slaughtered out back, the guests will be here in a few hours…

Frau Doctor stops him with a wave of her hand, twiddles the ribbon of her bonnet.

I am in agreement.

3

It didn't work out with the last maid because of the children, says Frau Tschudi as she leads Anna down the hall and into the kitchen. Stini was always complaining or gossiping and would whine with such self-pity, and for the slightest reason; but the children mean well. They may be a little exuberant, perhaps, but if you know how to handle them, then you'll have an easy time. She emphasizes that Anna must get along with the children, or else she will look for other help. To take a maid that is only partially useful would be utterly foolish!

Anna nods and runs her eyes over the copper pans, examining them for their thickness and cleanliness, and glancing from the red flickering lights to the oven, to the brass sieves, funnels, whisks, and ladles. She nods at what the Frau says, follows her to the window, and looks out over the courtyard and garden.

Because it is next to the town watch's training field, the garden is wide and deep, with greenery growing rampant all along the garden wall, forming a bulwark to the wild growth of trees and stubborn foliage. The scent of cinnamon from the yew tree wafts over to her.

There must be children out on the paved courtyard directly below the window. They can be heard laughing and shouting. Bending forward, Anna can only see a chopping block; she watches a hen fidgeting within the strong grip of a man's hand. The axe flashes in the sun, slashing down toward the hen's neck.

The children shriek.

That's old Jenni who lives at the wine presser's, finishing off the poultry. Such fun for the children, Frau Doctor says. I'll call the children in now. Only the three eldest are here. A neighbor took three-year-old Barbara and one-year-old Elsbeth on a walk to Ennetbühls; one must chase the sun much more here in Glarnerland than elsewhere.

She leans outside, calling: Züsi! Anna Migeli! Heiri!

Susanna, the oldest, comes first. Steinmüller prophesied that in two years she would be the prettiest girl in Glarus, and he could be right about that. How politely she brushes the hair out of her face before she offers her hand to Anna, how she nods at her with bright eyes. Already so big and sensible, Anna thinks, relieved. She has little experience with small children. Now the other two appear from the stairway, laughing and making a ruckus as they run into the kitchen tripping over each other.

Quiet down! Their mother puts her hands over her ears.

The four-year-old spreads his arms, makes flapping motions, and crows: All gone! Cock-a-doodle-doo!

Say hello, Heiri, his mother calls to him, but he jerks and waggles his head as if it were hanging off of his body by a single sinew.

Finally he calms down. After his mother repeats the order, he shoves his chubby hand at Anna. He is round and tanned quite brown, a cute boy. He will be a doctor like his father, Frau Tschudi says, but he still has time. And here, she nudges the second girl forward, is my second oldest, Anna Migeli or Anna Maria. I am not for corrupting the lovely, old-fashioned names, for saying Züsi instead of Susanna, for instance, but in Glarus the truncation of first names is common practice, so even I must constantly make an effort to pronounce their Christian names in their entirety.

That Anna Maria resembles Susanna is not to her advantage; unconsciously one sees her in the shadow of the older girl. Upon comparison all of her features appear a touch less vivid. Her eyes, her hair, even her face is less open and expressive. Observed alone she would be seen as a nice girl of eight or nine years, but in no way striking.

Heinrich, who is standing behind his sister, giggles and gives her a push from behind.

Anna Maria offers the maid her hand.

Anna lets go of it immediately; good Lord, she thinks. What was that rigid thing? Certainly not a hand, but a claw!

She almost shrieked aloud.

The chicken claw hidden in Anna Maria's sleeve falls to the floor.

Ashes! Ashes! We all fall down! Heinrich shrieks and rolls on the floor laughing.

The child has such an imagination, his mother says, shaking her head. Especially on föhn days like today the children drive me almost out of my mind. You had best go to your room now and get changed — you don't want to work in that skirt, do you? The Frau Doctor peers again at Anna's fashionable skirt.

Anna says that she has a work dress in her bag. The rest will be sent to the Steinmüllers' with the carriers from Werdenberg — yes, I have known the Steinmüllers a long time. I became friends with them when I worked for the bookbinder in Glarus. Yes, yes, he is a curious one, Steinmüller is. But they are good for conversation, both he and his wife Dorothea are; they are prudent, reliable people.

Your room? Five stories up. No, I have a headache and will not come along. The föhn wind is bothering me. And I was in childbed a month ago; it was a girl, stillborn. Susanna will show you to your room.

No, me! I want to! Anna Maria cries.

She runs up the stairs, Heinrich following her. He goes step by step with his little plump legs, holding onto the carved posts of the balustrade as he goes.

A typical maid's room. Anna has not been expecting anything else. In the attic, behind furniture and rubbish in storage, a narrow room weakly lit by a garret window. The bed seems much too big. It fills the room like a ship with rumpled sails.

The linens are dirty, they haven't been changed since Stini left, Susanna declares. Anna changes the bed. It looks as though Frau Doctor has not stepped foot in this room for a long time. Such air. Anna opens the window and lets the September air stream in. From inside it looks like the Glärnish mountain, with its configuration of cliff faces and fissures, is resting on her shoulders. She had hoped for this vantage point under the gable. If the children happen to be opening the drawers of the commode behind her back and taking out the keys, it is of no importance, she is across from the mountain just as she was back then in Mollis; she can settle things with him. Now she is certain it is good to be back, after all that hesitation two weeks ago.

4

No better time for traveling than mid-September.

The driver had pointed out the deer in the woods, fat and colorful, walking along the streams down into the gullies. Their hides look like rooster feathers, Anna thought.

It was lucky old Hilari was giving her a ride from Wattwil as he had once before; it would have been hard to make the climb to Hummelwald on foot. Sitting up front on the driver's bench with a mild wind breezing about her, she felt the journey was a holiday.

Cows grazed. Clappers swung back and forth in the bells hanging from leather bands about their necks. Staccato metallic tones hung over the fields. Here and there among the aftergrass stood an autumn crocus, strange and transparent.

Anna reluctantly acknowledged them as the harbingers of winter. The greater part of the year was gone; one must not be deceived by these late summer days, the shadows were growing. The blackberry tree, its sap boiling out in the last heat of the year, trembled at the prospect of frost.

Find yourself a home.

The horses trotted easily down the Rickenstrasse toward the hamlet of Schobingen until they were met by the lowlands crisscrossed by the Linth's watery threads.

Look how it sparkles, she said.

You think it's nice? Hilari responded with a laugh and wrinkled his nose, which was red and puffy from the many flasks of Veltliner wine he had sampled at inns and pubs along the road. This flat marshland is anything but nice. It brings plagues of mosquitoes and disease to the nearby villages. They've got to correct the river's course, but the people of Glarus would rather wait until the people of Schwyz agree to it and vice versa.

Near the village of Biäsche, across the Maag from Weesen, he stopped the horses on the bank of the river and told Anna she had better climb down since he was driving further on, along the Walensee to Walenstadt. Anna gave him a wave in thanks; then, gathering her skirts, stepped down from the footboard. She had long been using the trick of wearing three skirts, one over the other, so that everything else necessary for her journeys could be easily tucked away in a handbag. Göldin was clever when it came to traveling; hardly any woman of her class did this sort of thing. Out on the dusty roads, on foot or riding on a wagon, to Werdenberg, through St. Gallen and Glarus, then on to Strasbourg and now, after a detour to her home in the Rhine valley, back to Glarus. All these paths going here and running there, she was constantly fleeing the shadows that followed at her heels. She let the paths snap back into place like bands too tightly stretched. Reeds and willow trunks lined the road, the water shone behind.

A raft had run aground on a sandbar; the men aboard were poking with poles into the shallow water.

Hey, you want to come along? One called over.

Where are you going? She asked casually.

To Amsterdam in Holland.

Good heavens, so far? And on this little stream here?

At this, the other two men took a rest from their poling and looked over. The first, a blond with long hair, told her that they were starting here at the Walensee, going down the Maag, then down the Linth, and from there to the Zürichsee, down the Limmat, the Aare, and from the Aare to the Rhine. Where are you heading?

She pointed to the nearby mountains.

To Glarus? The three laughed. That's where we've come from — Elm and the Plattenberg. Beneath the surface of the mountain there are slabs of slate for tables, soon to be in Amsterdam's genteel houses!

That singing Glarus dialect.

Now it mixed sweetly with the lapping of waves. She had not heard it for a long time.

Consider it, maiden, said the smallest, who had a marmot's clever eyes. We'd be glad to make room for you.

Their tanned faces. Brief flashes of light through the mauve shadows of the reeds. The summer, previously thought lost, played at its game of hide and seek; a light wind from the lake brushed through the sedge and waterfowl took flight.

Anna's eyes, at first lost in the mountains, became lively and radiant. She stood there, her head tilted as if she were seriously considering the journey to Holland. She was a handsome person of good stature whose image could still awaken pleasant sensations, even if she were not so young anymore. Everything hung in the balance on this föhn day with its mother-of-pearl cast; she could still turn back and head for the broad plains on this sparkling cord of water.

But that valley yonder, that narrow gap between mountain faces exerted an inexplicable pull.

Reeled in like a fish on a line, dangling from a hook as she had back then when she escaped under duress through the only way out, the narrow passage at Mollis.

She could still turn back.

It was not to be. Hoof-clops sounded from the tollhouse. Automatically she raised her arm to wave at the approaching vehicle.

Clouds of dust. The horses snorted, impatient with the abrupt halt.

It was a rickety wagon covered with resin-infused fabric. The driver leaned out over her, his face shaded by the brim of his felt hat.

She recognized him! The mail carrier from Sargans. She had seen the driver before, his pipe held between damaged teeth, from the kitchen window of the Zwicki house, and sometimes his wagon could be found parked in front of the Inn of the Wild Man in Glarus.

He reached for her arm and pulled her up onto the seat.

Do you have only this little satchel with you? It looks just like a midwife's bag.

And it is one, too, said Anna, chuckling. My cousin, a midwife in Werdenberg, gave it to me.

So you're from Werdenberg, and a subject of the governor of Glarus?

I am indeed from the Rhine valley, but from the county Sax; it belongs to Zurich.

Then you are lucky, the driver said, there are no governors more wicked and bloodsucking than Glarnerland's. They get so little income from the people under them that they have to squeeze out bribes and levy fines to pay for their offices.

The road led southward through the lowlands to the mountains.

A stranger to the place would never suspect that a valley opened up behind the cliff wall. Nor that the mountains retreated further the closer one came, *Open Sesame*, making way for a road to squeeze in beside the Linth as well as a little bit of valley to the river's left and right.

The mail carrier pushed his pipe into the corner of his mouth to make room for a stream of words and the strong odor of goats. She let him talk and play tour guide, let him go on and on, over there is Mollis, and this is Näfels, he said. The castle, which attracts the eye of every stranger on the street, was built by a man named Freuler. He was a captain in Fontainebleau and took in money as if it were hay and had the *idée fixe* that the king of France would come to visit him. The king had promised to come, and all of the lower class believed it, but up among the lords and ladies another wind blew, and Freuler waited until he was old and poor, and doesn't it seem that the palace is still keeping lookout for the king?

She nodded absently, facing away from him to avoid the stench of goat. Her eyes climbed the harsh cliff walls of the Wiggis.

The Linth gurgled behind alder trees.

A filmy moon hung over Glarus, the canton's capital, beyond which the valley again narrowed.

A stately village, the driver remarked as they drove past the first houses toward the Spielhof. Cotton spinning has become quite popular. I've counted fourteen factories since Burghügel; they're shooting up like mushrooms lately here in town, with those exorbitant factory complexes on the Oberdorf stream and in the Abläsch and Insel neighborhoods.

They get cotton from Venice and sell the thread to Zurich, St. Gallen, and Appenzell. Major Streiff died recently; he apparently left one and a half tons of gold behind, a veritable gold mine, from his cotton and handkerchief printing. He made the majority of his money printing with a blue ink called indigo. Streiff didn't have a single son, so everything went to his son-in-law, the judge and councilman Johannes Tschudi…

Idle gossip.

In one ear and out the other.

From below on the seat of the wagon she greeted her Glarus. She was glad to see the elegant houses again, with their shingled roofs weighted with stone, and the stores, the arcades, the boutiques — here the wig maker's shop, there Freuler the goldsmith's, further on a new store with gourmet potables.

Money rolls through the streets of Glarus, she had thought when she came for the first time from the meager portions of Sax and Sennwald.

Father's voice from childhood in her ear: gold mining towns, Anni. You've got to make your own luck. I know some people from Toggenburg who've set off for Pennsylvania.

The hunt for everything that glitters, her preference for comfort, the fantasy of a city of gold: sleeping in a freezing bed yet dreaming of warm ovens.

After Father's death the debt collector took what there was to take.

Mother was always sending her to neighbors to request this and that. Yes, you, Anni.

Over there, under the stern eyes of the Riedbauers, clearing her throat, blushing, stammering questions:

May I borrow your pail?

Your wooden tub for washday?

Your spade?

Salt?

The watering can, the dibble, the rake, the ladder?

Sent away with their excuses: We need that ourselves, ask at the Kreuzbauers. Or: We're washing too, come again next week.

And when she came the next week, they had forgotten everything, starting over once again: What do you want? Can't you talk?

The tub?

Take it, but it must be back by evening, understood?

Lordy, the purest of beggars.

They drove by the church tower with the golden sundial, through the narrow lanes to the Adlerplatz.

Would you like to share a bottle of Veltliner wine with me? Anna turned down the offer.

She wanted to meet up with her friends in Glarus's Abläsch neighborhood before dark.

5

In one of the guest rooms of the Golden Adler, Johann Michael Afsprung, the scholar from Ulm, made an entry in his travel diary, which he would later publish under the title *Journey through a few cantons of the Swiss Confederation*. He wrote:

The mountains which enclose the charming valleys terrify; strolling between them one feels almost crushed by the view of these monstrous masses, for they wake in men the deepest feelings of impotence…

Anna's Glarus — that Glarus of 1780 — can still be glimpsed with the help of old prints.

On onc May night in 1861 it was almost completely burned to the ground. The reflection of the blaze on the mountains was visible from as far as Ravensburg in the Black Forest and Neuchâtel to the east.

The village was rebuilt according to the fashion of the second half of that century; they leveled the grassy moraine, called the *Tschudirain*. Now everything was open, a miniature town on a chessboard.

The cause of the fire was never discovered. It was said that the fire broke out in one of the houses on the Zaunplatz; someone must have left out an iron with glowing coals. A maid, a stranger, was blamed.

In the evening the dining room in the Tschudi house is lit with candles.

Their glow softens the chiseled profile of Colonel Paravicini, the imperious nostrils of Major General Marti and the cleft of his chin, smoothing the finely carved scholarly features to match those of the lawyer and former Chief Magistrate Cosmus Heer. Curving shoulders and décolletés shimmer in the light. Frau Paravicini's breasts rise out of her plunging neckline like half-moons. Involuntarily one thinks of the extravagant crest over the door of her estate, the "Alders": a white striding swan with a golden crown, and under it the gravure: *candidor nive,* "as white as snow."

Anna passes the platters around. That afternoon she found that the herb garden was overgrown and the scarce bushes were too old, moldering in the shadow of the wall, but with some oregano, parsley, and sage, she was able to make a *sauce verte* using one of her Zwicki recipes, and it is the subject of high compliments from the diners.

Among the ambitious, even daring assortment of guests, conversations proceed carefully and agreeably with superficial chatter that slips past dangerous themes like rocks in a riverbed. After dinner the men go into the host's study, leaving the women at the dining room table. Anna serves coffee from a silver pot.

A skirt with this season's colors, Frau Baronet Zwicki remarks, glancing over at Anna and raising a doll-sized cup to her mouth.

That shiny fabric is a *nouveauté* from Paris, they call it "*moiré,*" Frau Lieutenant Becker says.

Fashion is so *changeant*, Frau Councilman Marti tuts.

Did you know that Frau Becker from Ennenda goes to Paris for her clothing? Her husband runs a trading company in Brussels.

And such colors, says the Frau Baronet. The French call that one there "flea colored."

Mon dieu!

All the *couleurs* have such twisted names, Frau Lieutenant Becker continues. For example, there's "street grime," "nun's thigh," "monk's belly"… a green the color you are wearing, your Grace, and she indicated Frau Doctor Iseli's skirt, is called "smallpox," and an indefinable brown is "*caca du dauphin.*"

Dégoutant, coughs Frau Colonel Parvicini. Her eyes sparkle sea green under the fans of eyelashes she had artificially extended, the devil knows how. Frau Tschudi glances at her low-cut décolleté.

Shameless, that neckline. Frau Tschudi does not consider it prudent to attend a dinner party in such a revealing dress, particularly when the camerarius is also be there.

Frau Becker, noting her hostess's displeasure, tries to distract her with a general remark and, indicating Anna's skirt, says, ah, domestic help these days.

The sigh finds agreement. Frau Tschudi's eyes break away from the offending neckline.

The ladies nod.

Apparently the maid of Herr Marti, the owner of the Adler, gave some cheeky remarks before the court the other day, Frau Doctor Iseli comments.

What did she say?

The women's faces move closer, their eyes narrowing in appreciation.

Some men deserve to have their wigs pulled off…

When the maid enters the room of gentlemen, the conversation goes silent as if by chance. They watch her as she brings around cups and pours coffee.

A new maid? Doctor Marti asks after Anna has left again. The host nods. She previously served the Zwickis in Mollis.

Hence the exquisite cuisine, the camerarius states.

The Zwickis could have afforded to keep an extravagant inn, Captain Tschudi of the town watch remarks. In spite of his various activities — in fact, he had recently attempted to start up a small pub — he himself had gotten nowhere with that sort of thing.

Yes, the living in Bilten is in great demand, Cosmus Heer responds, but that's not how the pastor acquired his great wealth; someone in his family must have been well situated…

Such a rich pastor, Herr Marti, the old Augustinian, says quietly. Is that proper, when our Redeemer was poor?

Embarrassed silence. Winks.

It has spread around town that old Marti has become devout in his last days and is moving in Pietist circles. The host, his mouth pursed scornfully, looks over at the camerarius. Johann Jakob Tschudi, first pastor in Glarus, member of the Morals Court, chamberlain of the synod, cousin of Elsbeth Tschudi and godfather of Anna Migeli, is charged with answering such delicate questions.

The camerarius abruptly raises his hand so that his laced cuffs fly back dramatically, a movement he also tends to make during sermons. The guests sit back in their seats. Whenever the camerarius begins to speak, a long digression can be expected.

The Lorrrd…

The *r*'s shake the room as if a horse-drawn cart were driving over bumpy paving outside.

The crest with the Tschudi fir tree vibrates against the window.

The Lord favors His chosen ones, as Calvin preached. He bestows blessings and prosperity on their earthly affairs as He did once for Abraham in the Old Testament. God is with those who are active, clever, and wise. He gives them comfort and well being, even now in their earthly dwelling. This word "comfort" is from Old French and originally meant "to strengthen."

Cosmus Heer squints at the camerarius with eyes reddened from too much reading. He had established the archives of the canton and was chairman of the Glarus Literary Society and the Society of Helvetica. Well, if the blessings of God can be measured by one's portfolio, then He indeed rains them down on the Zwicki family, he remarks with that sort of mild sarcasm that never fails to annoy the camerarius. The Zwicki family fortune continues to grow through their advantageous unions. Their youngest daughter, Dorothee, has been married to Captain Conrad Schindler. He is building a home in the Haltli neighborhood of Mollis. Its elegance and grandeur surpasses the mansions of Glarus by far. And recently Captain Schindler won the Dutch state lottery — one hundred thousand guilder, believe it or not! A sum great enough to build three more palaces!

Money goes to money, mutters Captain Tschudi, aghast. One hundred thousand—and the rest of us are like schoolmasters duped into forty-two guilder a year!

The host throws him a censuring look. Time and again the doctor realizes he must take his young relative of few powerful connections off of the guest list. But at least the captain knows to show his gratitude with service. On the other hand, he also makes his insolent remarks in company and attracts attention with his faux pas. And the Frau Doctor always comes to the young man's defense.

Anna pours coffee.

The tiny porcelain cups, fit for dolls, are empty after only three sips.

To go back to the Zwickis in Mollis, says Doctor Marti, taking up the conversation again, our colleague, Melchior, is considering marriage.

At long last, says Doctor Iseli. He is almost forty, after all.

Doctor Marti nods. He's finally leaving his mother for the bonds of marriage. He has chosen the twenty-year-old daughter of Schindler, the church steward…

One of the small cups falls to the floor with a crash. Anna quickly bends down. Frau Tschudi hurries in from the next room and exclaims over it as one of her delicate and expensive Limoge cups, brought from Paris by her brother-in-law the lieutenant, and goes on to complain about the clumsiness of this and every maid. None of the men contradicts her.

Anna goes out of the room with the shards on the silver platter. The mistress follows her to the kitchen and says she will deduct a half guilder for the cup from Anna's salary at the end of the month. I would rather give you the half guilder immediately, Anna says calmly.

Later, back in the room of gentlemen, Doctor Marti asks Anna where she came from, as her dialect has a lighter sound than the local one. Then in response to her answer, he remarks that he knows her part of Sax well; he traveled through Sennwald last autumn on his way from Sargans to Lake Constance. The Zurich governors must be getting very little from that area. The people are poor and in debt. The Rhine lays waste to the low fields with floods, and the fields on the hillsides are full of stones.

6

In autumn, when the föhn wind blew through the Rhine valley, the milky grains on the corncobs hardened and the backs of children could bee seen among rustling leaves.

Adrian Göldi piled up the stones Anna and her siblings had gathered from the fields. He built dry stone walls; they were more suitable than wooden fences, which toppled easily under the weight of snow and then decayed in the rain-swept summers. The neighbors, too, piled up stones. The entire hillside, as far as the eye could see, was adorned with a continuous belt of stone, border on border, up to the foot of the mountain.

Adrian had not yet finished his wall when the governor in Forstegg sent a summons calling for workers to reroute a stream for a fountain in the castle.

Her father growled, I have to cut down some pear trees standing in the way of my new wall. Besides, I'm the church sexton.

The servant from the castle replied that the trees were not going anywhere. And you will have plenty of time to set up the pews on Saturday. Every subject owes the governor three days; there is no reprieve from this required labor.

Days that fly to and fro like chaff in the wind.

They have two sides. Like playing cards.

On the backside was the sign of the powers, incomprehensible.

That old prankster—death.

Smallpox.

Dysentery.

The lord at Forstegg.

Blazing fires, livestock plagues.

Rockslides from above, the Rhine below.

The Rhine was unpredictable during thaws and fall storms; whenever it flooded, the sexton had to ring the church bells. At the sound of the alarm, every man laid down his work and hurried over field and swamp. They gathered at the dam. The men of Sennwald were divided into groups; everyone had to contribute. On order of the governor. Anyone who refused was taken to Zurich.

And you, too, Adrian, said her mother. Give me the pitchfork, I'll do it myself. If you get to the dam late, you'll be fined six batzen.

Adrian threw down the pitchfork and searched for his boots on the threshing floor. He doesn't have a bit of food or drink with him, her mother lamented. Such a hot temper.

She planned to fill the sow's trough and clean out the sty. Then down to the Rhine with a basket of food. If she took the two younger girls along, then Katharina, her oldest, could watch over the place while she was gone.

Through rolling meadows down to the river valley, their toes in wooden shoes got wet from the grass. In the shadow of the mountain the ground was cold; frost bit at the earth amid the stubbly aftergrass.

Behind some alder bushes Anna discovered a stream, and in it a freckled fish.

Trout, her mother said. They belong to the governor. The stream is part of his property.

Does everything belong to the governor? Anna asked.

The land over there doesn't belong to him. Her mother pointed to the other side of the river, to Austria, to cloud-covered mountains that looked as if they were painted on a canvas.

Who does it belong to?

Another lord.

No, not through the swampland. It's treacherous, it will catch your feet and suck you in. Her mother preferred to go through the forest by Salez. But that, too, was spooky, full of boulders and shadows.

Her mother pulled her woolen three-corner shawl closer about her shoulders, and held onto her children at her right and left. They became dizzy as their eyes strayed up from the tree trunks to the Kreuzberg mountain. Clouds were moving between the Kreuzberg's prongs as if through a giant comb, and the girls almost fell over. Intermittently stones flew down the hillside and came to rest among beech and fir trees.

There were wagons in a forest clearing. Men were loading up tree trunks; the building of the dam ate up wood.

Anna stared down at the river, at its green foaming water. Overnight the Rhine had destroyed the old delapidated dam. All the men in the village, including the governor and his servants, had not been able to get the flooding in check.

Come along, Anni. What are you staring at? Look over there. See, it's Papa.

The men were ramming piles into the ground and filling the area between them with gravel and sand. The dam overseer was concerned with adhering to the *möni*, the established path for the river. No one was allowed to pinch off any of the land from the Rhine in one's own favor, or else it would cause quarrels such as it had recently, when the Austrian authorities charged that the people of Sennwald "did throw the Rhine with much force onto the meadows of Bangs."

In the evening, when her father came home exhausted, he lifted Anna into his arms, swung her around in a circle, and praised her. You good little girl, you went all that way for your Papa. He said it only to her, even though Barbara, her younger sister, also went along.

Anna, wide-eyed and with her father's wet kiss on her nose, looked closely at his cheek; it was stubbly and full of dark shadows, like the meadow in the shadow of the mountain.

Her father finished his wall. From a distance it looked like a snake moving through the grass, with gray spots and stony scales protruding from it here and there.

The neighbors had put up their walls, too. The hillsides lay there under November winds, long narrow fields and bits of meadow with stunted fruit trees. The sky hung low and the land awaited the snow.

To the child Anna, the house seemed large during the good times of the year, with expansive gables that bent upward on the ends like wings reaching out to grasp the threshing floor and stables below them.

It stood upon its narrow, whitewashed foundation, and its walls were of blackened wood. The little windows stood precisely aligned in three rows; in the Appenzell style, each window had a single shutter that could be pulled up out of a recess below.

In winter, when they needed to keep the warmth inside, the house looked as if it had no windows, as if its eyes were turned inward. When the snow and cold arrived, the house hunkered down, small and narrow. It shrank inside, too, concentrating itself in a single warm room.

Like all the poor people, her father took in livestock from Graubünden during the winter months so he could pay the rent on St. George's day. If their stores ran out, he would have to buy hay at high spring prices; better the people starve than the livestock.

The family gathered their sparse stocks together: potatoes, dried pear slices, cornmeal. Their main nourishment came from milk and whey. During the winter her mother spun wool to add a few kreuzer to their income. Her constant laments accompanied the whirring of the wheel.

She had a complaint for everything, even during summer, but then her rants merely blew away like smoke into the open sky. Now in winter everything stood hanging in the kitchen and made the air thick.

By contrast, Anna's papa remained lively even in winter. Sometimes in the afternoons he went out to the Protestant church, but his duties as sexton were not very demanding; aside from Wednesdays, when the pastor gave an evening sermon, the church was only used on Sundays.

On his way home he often stopped to visit some relatives who sold brandy. Sometimes the liquor went to his head, but he never became quarrelsome.

When he came home drunk, he tried to flatter and charm Anna's mother, who sat at the spinning wheel late into the night. He knew there was a way to sweeten her up, and Anna, unable to sleep, listened spellbound. A small flap into her room was left open to allow the heat from the stove to come in, and she peered through it into the living room. She watched with bated breath as her father put his hands on her mother's waist and pulled her from the wheel but her mother shook him off and hissed and bristled like a cat that has been petted against its fur's nap.

Hardly had her mother caught her breath than she tore into him. How can you coo and dance around like that when we are up to our ears in debt? You certainly aren't going to be re-elected sexton again, haven't you heard what people are saying about you? That you're too frivolous?

Her father laughed drily. What do I care about what people say? And after a pause, as the spinning wheel began turning again, he added, we could emigrate like my mother's relatives — remember they left Sennwald for Prussia in 1712? But I would rather go further, to Newfoundland or instance, or Carolina, Pennsylvania or Virginia!

At the mention of these exciting lands Anna's mouth and eyes opened wide.

But her mother only said bitterly, oh, bah, it's all a stupid dream.

To escape the monotony, to get away from the whirring of a wheel that climbs up only to fall again, and falls only to climb again, activity without a goal.

You're like your father, Anni. Here and yet not here.

I don't understand, Mother.

You're different. You want to get away, to leave. How can I say it any better than that? You're just a dreamer. But soon you'll see. Life will move you along.

Moved along, her feet steady on the Tschudi's parquet floor. Her hands, too, are reliable, attending to her work with purposeful movements. Wiping up dust, cleaning dishes, rubbing brass bare, breaking through the outer crust. Yes, without salve, without your magic salve, Steinmüller. Old nonsense in those magic books you let them foist on you at the markets.

Leaving a trail: the tracks of a peasant, a maid, a single woman.

Be true and honest, Anni, listen to the Lord, obey the Lord, do not stray an inch from God's path.

To escape from oneself, a moth that flies from the tulip's opening chalice at midnight, a blue streak of light, a will-o'-the-wisp.

Away and out. For your feet, as far as they will carry you, will always move upon this earth. And it belongs to them, Anni. It is measured out, divided, sold, and covered by buildings; the fate of the small towns with their forests and the paths through the meadows has long been determined.

7

You mustn't go through my things, Anna Maria! The maid bends down, whisks up a comb, a drawing, and some coins from the floor, and puts everything back in the box decorated with shells and mirrors.

The things in this room belong to me.

That's not true. It's our house. Our bed. Our commode. Our chair.

Anna pushes strands of hair from her forehead, and angrily closes the drawer, which remains crooked in its case. It can no longer be locked with its key.

Frau Doctor calls from below.

In the late afternoon Frau Tschudi sends Anna Göldin to buy two pounds of butter at the butter market. Anna loves to go outside more than anything after doing the housework, after languishing between cumbersome furniture, mirrors and bureaus, chasing down dust or being chased down by the mistress, who will suddenly show up and order the hallways, staircases and parquet floors as clean as a whistle.

On days like this she feels compelled outside, where the autumn light softens the sharp contours of the mountains and melts the shadows. The sun lays out slanting rays of light over the rusty tones of the Schwammhöhe forest. It would be nice to go down to the Linth. Along the dam, over the wooden bridges to Ennenda. She is jealous of old Frau Debrunner, who takes the two youngest Tschudi children on a walk everyday.

Anna takes off her apron in front of the hallway mirror, fishes with her little finger for the locks of hair caught under her bonnet, and pulls them down over her forehead.

The door to the dining room, where Frau Tschudi is having coffee with Frau Lieutenant Becker, is open a crack. A vain person, this Göldin, Frau Becker notes.

Frau Tschudi nods.

Anna cannot manage to go down the hall without looking in the mirror. She has a weakness for mirrors, for the trembling, blurry image that provokes the question: where do you begin, where do you end? The dismay of encountering one's own image, facing it in the twilit hallway: this is how you are, this way and no way else, yet you might have one hundred other faces than this one here, with dark hair curling over the brow, high cheekbones in a wide face, with gray, ever bright eyes that say they have been keeping watch for something that never came.

She never leaves the house without first examining herself, both back and front, Frau Tschudi says. Is she secretly waiting for someone to take her bait? We had Herr Leuzinger, the carpenter, come to the house the other day to fix the bookcase in the study. He flirted with her and she batted her eyelashes and became quite animated. Usually she goes around so absently, doing her work like she's sleepwalking. But she does do good work with her tasks, I cannot complain there…

Eyes that let you see yourself as others see you. Constantly re-created in other's eyes: now this Anna, now that one, this way and that way, as if someone were turning that amusing object, the kaleidoscope, with its colored shards falling one over the other.

Get going, Anna. You still have to preserve the plums today. Frau Tschudi has come out of the dining room; her image is now beside Anna's, framed by the oval of the mirror. A protruding, waxy forehead, dark wrinkles about her mouth, pale lips, as if there were no life, no blood within. As if etched on the mirror's glass by an artist … except for her eyes lurking in their shadowy nests.

Right away, says Anna.

Me too! Anna Maria cries from the next room. Me too! Heinrich crows, letting his hobbyhorse fall in the middle of the hallway and running to Anna.

Frau Tschudi pulls the little boy to her and wipes his nose with a laced handkerchief.

You stay here, Heiri. The Frau Lieutenant has a sugared almond for you.

But I wanna go with Anna! He wriggles out of her arms and stamps his foot.

You're staying. I will not tolerate you going out all the time. The evenings have already turned cold. And Anna Maria — have you learned the questions in the Catechism?

Anna Maria nods. Anna had me say them to her while she ironed the wash, and now I can say it all by heart: What is thy only comfort in life and death? Answer: that after this dismal life I will inherit everlasting joy and bliss and have eternal life with God my Father and be blessed with His heavenly goods. Break. How many things are in this answer? Answer: there are two things in this answer, first, my sins…

Tired, Frau Tschudi waves her away. One must always be on top of things with Anna Maria. Even Steinmüller the schoolmaster says so. But Susanna — the complete opposite. She picks up on everything immediately. So unfortunate she is a girl, she would have been a brilliant lawyer, even the camerarius agrees…

Doctor Tschudi, coming out of his office for a cup of coffee, has caught the last sentence. Yes, yes, he says and looks at Anna Maria for a moment. Try to follow your older sister's example.

Then he laughs his rumbling earthy laugh; the girl stands there and stares at him, her lips pressed together into a thin line. Now she looks exactly like her mother in the mirror.

Time to go now, Frau Tschudi commands. After dinner the fruit has to be pitted. A farmer from Rieden gave the baskets to the doctor for curing his feet. The plums are already soft and will start molding soon.

The sun has gone down outside, but its rays are still shining on the rocky tip of the Wiggis. Carts roll down the main street and some travelers are stepping out of a coach in front of the Golden Adler. There are still some stalls set up at the butter market. The fountain gurgles behind a farmer's wife boasting about her eggs, which she had hoped to sell before dark. Large, guaranteed fresh… Oh yes, no older than yesterday.

Anna is interested. But every week Frau Tschudi buys them from an egg man from Kleintal. His eggs are never fresh, but they are inexpensive. The farmer's wife hands the ball of butter across the counter, and as Anna puts it in her basket, her elbow hits a man as he is bending down to pick something up. Why, Ruedi Steinmüller, she cries out in surprise. Are you looking for something?

He stands up, but as he straightens, he does not get much taller. He looks more like a gnarled grapevine root standing there than a man, on crooked legs and holding a Lindauer pipe in the corner of his mouth. What a whimsical old man! Anna Maria stares at him. No, she's never seen him before, though he greets her like an old friend, even asserting that he is distantly related to her. What, this crooked little man related to her, Anna Maria Tschudi, daughter of the doctor and judge!

I was picking up a stone, he tells Anna. It's been lying here for weeks. A boy from Kleintal pointed it out to me. It comes from a particular type of boulder. If you split this sort of stone, you'll find gold grains in it like in actinolite. I'm going to take it home now and take a look at it.

And there will be gold in it and you'll be rich, Steinmüller! Anna exclaims playfully.

You can never tell. Steinmüller spits tobacco juice on the ground. I'm just a dabbler, you know that. I try out all sorts of recipes in my laboratory. You might be interested in some of them. But we can do that, and he winks, indicating the child, another time.

What? Anna Maria cries. What did he say? Is there gold in the stone? Where? I want to see it! The child purses her lips, turns bright red, and kicks Anna's leg with her boot.

Oh, you nuisance! I must get home, as you can see. Has the trunk with my clothing arrived yet?

Steinmüller says that it has not. The messenger from Werdenberg recently started coming on Friday only. I'll have it delivered to you when it arrives.

Mist has settled on the Adlerplatz. A man wearing a coat with a beaver collar steps out of the brightly lit inn and stops in front of Anna. He runs his hand over the child's blond hair and peers into the maid's face. Are you Anna Göldin?

He bears greetings from the Frau Pastor Zwicki in Mollis. And Doctor Melchior Zwicki sends his greetings as well.

Heat shoots from her throat into her cheeks. She nods but does not make a sound.

Who was that? Anna Maria asks as they move on.

I was going to ask you that, the maid replies.

She almost has to pull the child along, who is walking pensively through the arcade and singing:

To my garden I will go
To tend my honey bees,
A wee old hunchback awaits me there,
My flowers make him sneeze.
To my kitchen I will go
To cook a tasty fish,
A wee old hunchback awaits me there,
He broke my favorite dish.
To my attic I will go…
What are you singing? The maid asks.

Just a song that Stini, the maid before you, sang to me. She told me ghost stories, too. Of Ursus, who is buried on the men's side in the church. He gave away his land a long time ago. Know who he gave it to? To Fridolin, of all people. You know, that barefoot man on the Glarus banner, the one holding the Bible. But when Ursus died, his brother Landolf wanted the land. So Fridolin went to the grave and called out, Ursus, arise!

And you know, Anni, the corpse came out of his coffin and helped Fridolin… have you ever seen a ghost, Anni?

Anna laughs. Never a ghost, but in the church in Sennwald there is a mummy of Count Philipp of Hohensax. He's been dead for one hundred and fifty years, killed by a relative. And he has lain there undecayed in his coffin ever since. My father was the sexton. He opened the coffin for me.

Was it a miracle, Anni?

No, they merely put him in some special soil.

Could I see him?

If you came with me to Sennwald, you could.

Anni?

Yes?

Anna Maria pulls on her arm like it's a bell-rope.

Have you ever seen a dead body — a real one, I mean?

Yes. My father, three of my siblings, Pastor Zwicki…

Do they simply lie there stiff, when they're dead?

The body is empty like a peapod. Whatever was inside has fled.

Which hole does it come out of?

Out of the mouth, I think.

And then the living stand around the bed and cry until their eyes are red?

Yes, mostly.

Then I would like to squint my eyes a little and look around, Anni, when I'm dead, I mean.

You silly girl.

8

I am in excellent health, wrote Pastor Zwicki to his friend in Zurich, and hardly had he strewn sand on the letter than he fell over dead.

A splendid, staunch young fellow, people in Sennwald had noted, and three days later, Anna's brother Hans was stricken dead by dysentery.

Death, a very busy grim reaper. When everything is silent, he can be heard sharpening his scythe.

We are born to die, and we die to eternal life, the camerarius said in his most recent sermon. The dead are near to us, not carried away to some far-off heaven. I feel them both near to me, my two wives now sleeping in the Lord, Anna Blumer and Anna Dinner, and the camerarius had suddenly pointed upward, as if he were vaguely indicating the whereabouts of Anna 1 and Anna 2.

Anna imagined this from her pew, the dead below, thousands and thousands of dead who were in Glarnerland before, deposited like boulders at the foot of the mountains, and only a handful of lives in the valley.

Protect those few who still live. The dead increase their numbers daily.

At the end of February, as the thaw set in, her papa pulled the horn sled from the threshing floor and took it out over the fields of Sennwald into the woods. The forest was dark; between the tree trunks the pale ground was visible as if through sparse animal fur. Ice melted from the branches. The drops froze on the shadowy ground and wove a shining blanket with the previous year's foliage.

Hardly had her papa loaded up a pile of wood in the upper barn than the sled began to slide downhill. He turned his back to it and tried to halt its progress, his hobnail boots skidding under him, but the sled continued to push him along down toward the valley; further down he managed to brace himself with his legs against a beech tree. He would have been crushed by his load of wood otherwise. It gently slid away, leaving one wound gaping open on his left knee.

Her papa didn't worry about it.

He had often gotten worse-looking cuts while chopping, mowing, or downing trees. In the stable he smeared warm cow dung on it and wrapped a cloth around his knee. But the usually-effective remedy was useless this time. His knee began to pulse. It swelled up and finally Anna's papa had to hobble around the house one-legged.

Her mother scraped the cow dung from the wound. By evening of the next day, heat had risen up his body from the wound. Her papa had to stay in bed and in the morning was speaking confusedly. At times he cried out as if he were dreaming and demanded water.

Her mother called for the doctor, but he was delivering a child at one of the cottages in Ried. When he finally came, her father lay breathing weakly in the dim room. Too late, the doctor said, you should have called for me sooner. Anna was sent for the pastor. The return trip seemed an eternity to her. One side of old Pastor Danuser's body was crippled. With effort he pulled himself along by his cane, tapping as he went with Anna down the path. She was freezing in her thin coat. The fruit trees were blue in the twilight; they seemed to shiver from the frost. When they finally reached the sick man's room, Katharina was there, her oldest sister who was serving in Salez at the Adler Inn. Andreas her brother was absent. He was a farm laborer in faraway Meyenfeldt. The pastor sat down and opened *The Musical Halleluja* on his knees, the hymnal of the Evangelical Church of the Confederation. He paged through it and found Chapter CCCLI. Bittersweet death, he read aloud. The others, now kneeling around the sickbed, murmured along with him:

> O, how bitter is death
> When body and soul must part
> But look straight to Him
> He leads us from our need
> So we might also say:
> O, how sweet is death

The mumbling quieted, then swelled imploringly. Anna's eyes filled with tears, behind which her father's bed seemed to float away.

> How bitter is death
> When we must leave this world
> One as red as roses today
> Tomorrow could fade away…

Her father, now a stranger, lay with a forbidding expression on his rigid face, his eyes wide open, focused on the ceiling as if he could see the night sky through the wooden beams.

> But what are we here
> But earth and filth

By and by we will blossom there
How sweet is —

Papa! Anna sobbed. The pastor, her mother, and her sisters glanced at Anna, and the prayer faltered. Her mother hushed her and steered her to the pastor, who laid his hand on her head.

9

At bedtime Anna Maria loudly calls for Anni to come up to say goodnight to her. The Frau Doctor, intimidated by the scathing glare of the child, tries to remain firm. No, she emphasizes, the maid cannot come, she's preserving plums in the kitchen. The child arches her torso back and shrieks: Anna! Anna!

Frau Tschudi turns to her husband, who is sitting on Susanna's bed.

Say something!

At his wife's demanding tone, his face takes on a baffled expression. He scratches his head, moving aside the wig at his hairline to reach his scalp and ample, curly hair.

The children are attached on the new maid, he says placatingly. She has a nice way about her and she is neither too lax nor too harsh in handling them, it seems to me. It might be good for you so you can relax a little.

But this is entirely the wrong thing to say to his wife. What is too much, is too much, she remarks sharply. The maid is binding the children to her in a way I am not entirely at ease with, in any case.

Tschudi rests his chin in his hand and massages his pasty cheeks with his fingertips. When he lets go, small indentations remain, imprints as on an overripe fruit. One can never make things right for the female sex, he thinks. Plato determined long ago that her moodiness came from her womb. It is always craving another child, almost before it has been delivered of the last one. His Elsbeth is particularly susceptible. Married in 1769, and already her tenth delivery in 1780. He thinks with a touch of exhilaration of the unrefined words of his farmer patients who come to his practice and enviously lament that he only needs to hang his underwear on his wife's bed — and tada! She is pregnant.

He is currently in the habit of going into his study in the evening to drink some Meyenfeldter wine and read until he is tired enough for sleep, then curling up next to his sleeping spouse on his side of their matrimonial bed.

Those stupid plums, what hogwash that they would go moldy. That is two basketsful to be cut up in the dim light, then pitted, cooked in portions with sugar, skimmed with a ladle, and poured into stoneware jars, which must then be sealed with slices of wax. And finally the hearth has to be scoured, as well as the floor. Everything is sprayed red, as after a battle.

She takes her small sweet revenge in the kitchen when everyone is asleep. She cuts a piece of white bread, which is only for her employers to enjoy, strews it with treats: butter, sugar, cinnamon, and hazelnuts. Almonds rolled in hot, caramelized sugar. A slice of smoked sausage. Several gulps of raspberry brandy. Sweet on sour. A delicious remedy for counteracting fury.

In his *Manuscript for Servants*, which Frau Zwicki in Mollis had given Anna, Lavater warned against "little meals prepared in secret."

Can this be? You are not familiar with the name Lavater, Anna? *Mon dieu*, I do not understand this, Frau Zwicki said back then. But you served in Sennwald with a pastor from Zurich, did you not? He preferred heathens, you say? Greeks? By my soul, I cannot even begin with such fashionable foolery. With Lavater there is heart, feelings, and the power of language. Potent in its bulk and breadth. But what am I saying to you, Anna? Sometimes I speak with you as if you were my peer, above all since my Johann Heinrich is no longer here. That happens when people live so long at such close quarters; then their differences retreat and commonalities step forward. (At this, Melchoir looked across the table at Anna. Do you hear that, his look meant. We can have hope. She thinks like us.)

My husband and I visited Lavater in Zurich, when he was still an assistant in the church orphanage. Because of him Zurich has now become a place of pilgrimage for many spirits. Goethe, by the way, discussed Lavater's *Prospects for Eternity* in the *Frankfurt Review of Books*.

That Anna had never heard of Goethe was less surprising to Frau Zwicki.

As she climbs the steps everything is silent. Only the doctor's study still has light shining from it. In her room, Anna takes out Lavater's text from the drawer of her nightstand, opens it with fingers stained red from plum juice, and reads in the flickering candlelight.

God's guiding Providence desired that thou shouldst be a servant, and that thou shouldst extend thy power of service and help to other people. Everything that God wants is good. It is better that thou shouldst be a servant or maid than anything else. It is God's will that thou servest others, who according to their outward circumstances are higher than thee — as God has called each, thus he transforms —

Behave in all naivety, as thou couldst require of a servant in all fairness, if thou wert the master!

Be also happy with a small reward, and not envious nor suspicious! God is thy reward — and heaven thy hope, if here below thou dost good work and have patience…

Anna yawns and douses the flame.

Waking, sleeping, and a dreamless half-waking, intertwined. But a sound has suddenly roused her. Lying on her back, her eyes wide, she listens. Steps outside in the attic, the door creaks open, a shadow slips in, sweeps along the bed…

Good Lord! Anna abruptly sits up. Is that you, Anna Migeli?

Yes.

There are birds with blue wings in my room. They're flapping all around. And Philipp the mummy opened up his coffin…

Anna sternly tells her to go to her mother.

But we aren't allowed to bother her behind her bed curtains. She'll be angry and send me back to my room. And Father snores like the wolf in fairy tales.

Please, please, let me sleep with you, Anni.

One should never tell children of gruesome things, neither of death nor spirits, witches, nor devils, warns Lavater in his book for servants. Or there will be trouble.

She moves over.

This maid's bed is an animal den.

With pits and clumps of wet, lumpy seaweed.

The room is still dark, sheltered by the night bird's wing; the darkness rustles. The girl's body gradually warms. The maid can feel the soft belly under her clasped hands.

Her head secure in the crook of Anna's chin, the child has no idea that her defender is defenseless. Memories. She grows wings like a woman in Diana's train. Anna, the bird of the night. Carving the darkness of night. The speed of thoughts. Angular houses take shape, the noises of wheelbarrows sound in the streets. Strasbourg. Then she herself steps out of the shadows and walks down the street, into one of the timberframe houses and presses a blond child to her, her mouth against his head, which smells of nuts. Her breath blows eddies in his hair.

His little legs are too gaunt, please put more butter in his porridge.

More boarding fees? Fine. Tomorrow I'll ask my employers to raise my wages. (What does Lavater know anyway, sitting at his desk in his happy little home or standing at his pulpit, of maids who must live hand to mouth trying to support a child conceived in the maid's chamber?)

Give me more money for his board, repeats the fat person behind her and laughs derisively.

I mean no offence, but you should keep him cleaner, too. (He is the son of a gentleman, a Zwicki. What sort of a town is this, where the name Zwicki makes no impression?)

Then care for him yourself, the wet nurse snaps.

You try finding employers that will hire a maid with a child, Anna wants to scream in her face. She knows well that the upper class will not take a maid with a child; they prefer to turn her into one. Men want the grass on the other side of the fence, but it mustn't cost them anything, she had said to Melchior outright, and as he went to get his wallet, she waved it away. Even prostitutes, who take money for each visit, would be less expensive. Much more expensive is a woman in whom emotions stir, for later life will also stir within her. This had not been taken into consideration; everything was supposed to run its natural course alongside his career, plans for the future, and wife.

Everything will change when the new time comes, Melchior had said. The new time, it's coming, it's coming.

It's not coming, Melchior.

There are definite signs in France and England that it is on its way.

Your new time — how long will it take to arrive? Before it even comes into the world, it has reached old age and wears wigs and plaits.

It's coming, you'll see.

Too late for you, me, and our child.

He's a bright lad. What is his name?

Melchior.

Strange name. The child is coughing. Look to him. I knew a child at this tender age who coughed his soul right out of his body…

Shrugging off the dream as if it is a clinging plant, moving out of the brown resonant twilight onto dry land. Morning light shoots through cracks in the shutters.

Anna Maria! She shakes the child and realizes in shock that the child's hair is wet from her tears.

I have to go down to the kitchen to start the fire.

She carries the drowsy child downstairs, lays her in her bed, and pulls the laced sheet evenly over her chest. I'll come to wake you soon, you have to go to school.

But I don't want to.

Well, you must, of course.

I don't have to do anything I don't want to.

But you must.

No.

The day begins with hesitation.

Shadows remain nestled at the back of the hearth. The masters sleep. Hard work pays off, the early bird gets the worm. Mottos for the common folk: they must bow to the inevitable, and so they give it a halo.

Frau Zwicki explained the God-ordained order in comparison to a cane: the ferrule down in the dirt, the silver knob above in God's hand. There were enlightened Libertines debating this in the Paris Salons, trying to overturn the existing hierarchies, the worthy below, the dirt above. All chaos — all of it, Anna — comes from the devil.

Anna has her own way of asserting herself.

Inch by inch she takes possession of her employers' home. And even if she never gets to relax in the flowery armchair, she still knows the degree of its tilt from taking a cloth dipped in olive oil to it. She dreams of the star-pattern of the parquet flooring, which she polishes with beeswax. She knows its gaps and cracks and the place in front of the tiled stove where two precious wooden slats are missing.

Anna Maria is not going to school today, Doctor Tschudi tells the maid that morning as she brings his coffee into the dining room. On account of one of those wretched headaches brought on by the föhn wind. Almost everyone in Glarus suffers from them. Even my wife is staying in bed this morning. Please sit down and drink a cup of coffee with me.

At first she feels some shyness about sitting at the table with an employer, whom she otherwise serves from platters, along with the unusual friendliness with which he turns to her and speaks of the herb garden. You might fix it up and fill it out with plants of your choice. I sensed immediately that you understand something of gardening.

Oh, I only acquired what familiarity I have with it from my cousin. She is a midwife in Werdenberg, Anna says humbly.

Such women often understand more of medicinal substances than doctors do, he admits and beams with his plump face in its frame of dark curls. He has not put on his uncomfortable wig yet, which never sits quite right over his stubborn hair.

Hardly has he gone into his office when the Frau Doctor calls from above.

Anniiii!

Thou shouldst respond the first time they call for thee… The voice of thy employer, so long as they do not mean thee ill, should be as the voice of God unto thee…

Anna leaves the dishes in the kitchen and goes upstairs. The bed curtains are pushed aside and Frau Tschudi, staring in abandon at a painting of a Tschudi ancestor on the wall, is lying there pale in her white damask dressing gown and sleeping bonnet.

Coffee, Anni. A lot of strong coffee. Put double the usual amount of beans in the mill.

Since she began serving in Glarnerland, she may as well clamp her knees around the coffee mill the entire day. Shocking really, how much of this Turkish brew the women of Glarus drink. They claim it chases away the fog in their heads that the föhn winds bring and illuminates their thoughts.

Anna nods and the Frau Doctor, her hands clasped over her face, listens to the sound of the maid's retreating steps. Through the open connecting door to the children's room, she hears Anna Maria's soft chanting:

To my chamber I will go
To make my bed of wicker
A wee old hunchback awaits me there
And then he starts to snicker…
Mama, can you hear me?
Yes.

Why isn't Anni poor like other maids are? Why does she have so much money up there in her dresser? And she has a little silver mirror with an angel on the handle, too. And in a little box she keeps a Bettli with a shell on it — you know, a velvet ribbon for her neck. I want one just like it. Maybe she's not really a maid at all, she only pretends to be. What do you think?

Of course Anna is a maid. An ordinary one like Stini.

The child seems satisfied with her answer. The woman lies there, looks at the ceiling, and waits for coffee, unaware of how the household is slipping away from her.

She thinks: Anna Maria notices more than others do, though people have long said that she not bright. Even my husband perpetually draws comparisons with Susanna. Listen, she had angrily said to him recently, the future will tell who the brighter one is. The younger is still struggling, but you'll see.

Well, yes, of course it is possible that things will still click with Anna Maria. She is just slow to comprehend, an Ellmer family trait.

She had glared at him with a deeply furrowed brow and spots appeared on her cheeks. Shall I tell you what people say? Fine, I'll just tell you frankly. That you became a doctor merely because your father was one, and that your father's purse was a big as your head.

If that were the case, my office would be empty, he responded patiently.

She finds it annoying that he never loses his temper, that he is so spineless. What a simpleton.

Anna brings in the coffee, a small pot of honey, and a few slices of white bread toasted in butter.

Here you are, Frau Doctor.

In the next room Anna Maria is given a cup of steaming chocolate. A maid like her doesn't have a bad life, thinks Frau Tschudi, watching Anna go. From the bed the maid looks more elegant than ever, well nourished and fresh with her full dark hair and rosy cheeks.

She can move around without attachment, whereas a woman in my standing must always take her husband and children into consideration. How she presents herself, so self-aware, with eyes that begin to sparkle whenever they come into the presence of a man, and the black adders of hair under her bonnet, *accroche-coeur*, or so the Parisians call those perky curls about the forehead.

Day and night, a woman of my standing must do whatever her husband wants, even in bed. She had barely turned sixteen when he got her pregnant and they had to get married as quick as lightning. The baby would have been crying in its cradle on her seventeenth birthday if

God had not taken it into His host of angels. And from then on she'd had no respite from pregnancy and birth. No more, she had said to him after the tenth birth. Or do you want the childbed to be my deathbed?

How strange, her friend Frau Lieutenant Becker recently whispered to her. Your husband is a doctor and should know what to do. There are positions that make you less likely to conceive as well as douches and herbal concoctions for aborting a baby.

You may not take any pleasure in it, her mother had warned her before the wedding, or you will not conceive. A wife must give herself without emotion, a virtuous hostess to a horny animal. The advice was worthless.

A belly that continually fills and bulges anew. Nine months full of complaints, waiting for the day, for the end of the period set by God.

Then that day when the bedroom was closed, when it was filled with the busy coming and going of women, when the doctor was allowed to stick his head in once in a while at most. Birth, women's business. Moans and shrieks carrying from the room to the rest of the house, where the children paused for a moment, then went on with their playing. They were told that the stork had bitten Mama's leg.

A kettle with warm water was already prepared for the first bath. Diapers, tiny camisoles with frills and ribbons, and receiving blankets. But the midwife saw immediately how weak the newborn was. They had better call for the camerarius right away, the little one will not last long. Indeed, she breathed her last before the pastor arrived. An unfortunate turn, for the unbaptized have neither rank nor name in heaven. The camerarius pressed the mother's hand, then upon returning home wrote in his book: August 13, 1780, Tschudi daughter, unbaptized, obiit, and next to it he drew a small cross.

One of the women put away the small clothing and cradle, and the carpenter brought the child's coffin to the back entrance. There were always a few set aside at the carpenter's workshop. In the parlor the little body was placed in the coffin. His mother had been through enough; she should not see it.

Ten born; five for the cradle, five for the coffin.

Anna, the coffee is too weak.

But Frau Doctor…

You should not always be saying *but*, Anna.

Anna is here for the house, not for the herb garden. I must make this clear once and for all, says Frau Tschudi. Besides, the garden in such a wild state is a thorn in my eye. It's obvious what is *à la mode* these days, all you have to do is look to the gardens of the modern upper class.

I've had enough of the jumble of weeds, the sharp smells along the wall, and those tree branches shooting out in all directions, taking up all the sun. I'm going to ask Captain Tschudi to take care of the yew and clip off all those branches that hit the wall. He can cut back the wild growth into artistic shapes: spheres, pyramids, and rooster heads. I want the garden neatly arranged, and the beds separated by a web of white gravel paths and low boxwood trees.

What? You'd rather keep the herbs in the garden and add even more herbs to the bunch?

Don't make me laugh.

You're not one of those herbalists who can do nothing more than brew concoctions for treating colic and headaches.

How backward that would be for a doctor who earned his diploma in Kassel, not to mention unworthy of your status! Anyway, there is already an apothecary nearby, that young Steinmüller. Leave all that to him. He and his assistant have a respectable supply of powders, pills, and proven medicinal remedies.

10

Don't ask so many questions, says the maid, pulling the child along down the main street to Abläsch, where there are branches burning in the last fires of summer on the banks of the Giessenbach. The mountains beyond have turned gray, foretelling winter storms.

Tell me, does he make gold, this Ruedi Steinmüller?

Nonsense, if he could do that he would be rich. He wouldn't have to be a locksmith anymore, toiling and sweating at the fire.

But aren't there little men who can make gold in fairytales?

Gnomes and dwarves, certainly.

She would have preferred to go alone to see Steinmüller, who has sent her word that her trunk arrived, but the child begged, please Anna, take me with you. And then she did not have the heart to leave her alone. Susanna had been allowed to go out with her mother for tea. A curtsey here, a curtsey there, her head tilted to the side, a polite laugh, all dressed up, her little doll in her petticoat, her hair spread over her lacy collar like a silk scarf. Next time, Anna Migeli, oh yes, certainly. Stay home and eat sugared almonds.

She is taking the girl on the condition that she not say anything of it to her mother. Frau Tschudi does not want the children to consort in houses of lower standing. Even distant relatives are not allowed an exception.

Steinmüller steps out of his workshop. I'm the only one here, my wife is with a niece in Riedern. You can go on inside, your trunk is in the parlor.

I was afraid the trunk was not going to come at all, Anna says to Steinmüller. In subject territories, your possessions are never completely secure. The Zurich governor is insatiable, confiscating whatever falls into his hands. It happened to me once with a trunk full of clothing I had sent back home from Mollis. The governors of such regions consider even the people their property, root and branch.

Anna opens the trunk on the parlor floor to check that everything is there. The child is kneeling beside her and softly strokes the fabric. Is this silk, Anna? And is that brocade? Anna nods as her glance slides rapturously over the fabric. She answers distractedly, envisioning herself walking among the stands at the St. Gallus market in one of these dresses the next day.

Once the trunk is closed again, Steinmüller comes in. He pats Anna Maria's head and gives her a picture for her prayer book, a silhouette of a gravestone next to a weeping willow with birds on it. A woman whose chronic bronchitis he cured with his honey paste cut it for him. He takes a book with metal clasps down from the bookcase. The creation story is in it. Can you read, Anna Migeli?

I can only copy down letters and spell them out.

Steinmüller nods, then remarks that judging by her age she'll be reading soon. But I know my cousin, the old schoolmaster, is squeezing two hundred children into one room and teaches without separating them into classes. Too bad the people of Glarus regretted spending the money to appoint two Protestant teachers, the Herrs Steinmüller, a father and son. Now the son has to make his livelihood with private lessons and an apothecary, where he also has to do the bookkeeping. Small wonder that the children advance at such a snail's pace in a school like that.

Why don't you look through the book, Anna Maria? There are some fine copper plates in it of the animals in Paradise, the Flood, and the tower of Babel. And while the child is looking at the plates, Anna, you might come with me to the smithy. I want to show you something.

In the smithy he pulls out a book from behind some glassware. There are secret recipes inside. I bought it for a dear price at the market in Weesen. I have to keep it hidden from Dorothea, she isn't understanding about my passion for these experiments. She'd rather see me following my day-to-day tasks like everyone else. But I certainly do whatever my job requires of me and I always please my customers. I am even trusted with journeymen. But after closing time I indulge my love of rarities. I would have liked to become a doctor of medicine or at least a barber, but my father did not have the money to pay my tuition. The canton scholarships were only awarded to the sons of rich men; they allowed the students to study at any price, no matter how idiotic any of the young men were individually. They could go to London, Göttingen, Kassel, Padua, and God knows where else. But a career in medicine requires talent, and if one is lacking there, then no amount of studying can make you successful. You can see that in your employer. Herr

Tschudi spent three years treating the injured leg of a carpenter who lived outside of Höfli. He tried all sorts of treatments, without success! I managed to find a cure for the carpenter's leg after trying for only two weeks. Thanks to a special salve, whose ingredients I will not reveal. Don't repeat a word of this. I don't want people to start talking about me. I'd rather live unnoticed and unobtrusive: envy is a terrible thing.

Anna suppresses a smile with effort. This curious little man, nimbly leaping like a coiled spring from her to the fire, from fire to the glassware, from the glassware to her and giving himself airs before her!

He opens the recipe book and holds it close under her nose. This recipe book was so costly because of the forbidden things printed in it: devil's coercions that will summon Lucifer, Beelzebub, Astaroth and others of Hell's princes, and it also reveals the signatures and sigils of the eighteen main spirits. He leaves his finger on the page. This is tricky, you're walking a tightrope with your legs dangling over the abyss of Hell. Have you heard what happened to the medical student on Christmas Eve in 1715? You can read a historic and detailed account of the incident in this book. Oh, I've got to go stir the cauldron…

Anna has trouble reading in the dim smithy, so she takes the book closer to the window. A medical student, assisted by two farmhands, had searched for treasure using magic. All three died in a little hut in a vineyard. An illustration depicts the soulless bodies of the student and the farm boys from Döbritschen and Ammerbach.

A strange affair. Very curious, very grim, murmurs Steinmüller, who now is standing next to her looking at the picture. But I would never get involved in anything like that. I'm interested in other recipes; a remedy for St. Anthony's Fire, for instance, which I've already tried out on a patient, and another one against worms that I'm brewing right now. It's a *spiritus urinosus*.

He shows her a test tube full of an oily, yellow liquid. You just chop up a snake and beaver testicles and dry the pieces outside in the sun with the blood of a baby goat. Then you distill that all down in a glass retort over a gentle fire. First the phlegm disappears, then the mucus, and after that the *sal volatile* settles like snow on the recipe pages. A certain smell steams out as long as the dark oil keeps dripping. But the *spiritus urinosus*, which has to be extracted from the oil, is separated by adding burned bone…

Lord! The child!

She is standing there in the dark, dank workshop, holding a dried frog in her hand. How long has she been standing there behind them? Anna should have known that the girl is impatient and would quickly be done with the copper plates.

Is it dead, Anni? I want to go home.

Steinmüller has slammed the book shut in alarm. As Anna leaves with the child, he hides it again behind the glassware.

They make their way home with the trunk.

The wind comes up and leaves swirl over the square. You have so many lovely clothes, Anna, says the child. So you've never been poor?

Oh, I have certainly been poor, you funny girl.

11

Back then, when they lost their father, provider, and source of income, their standing in Sennwald quickly went downhill. Hardly was her father in the ground when a servant from the castle came on the orders of the governor to inspect the stables. It was the custom that after the death of one of his subjects, the governor was given the so-called *fall*, the best livestock in the stables. There were not many to boast of, the single healthy cow being Lisetta, and the castle servant led her away.

Her mother had begged him to no avail to leave them the cow until spring; their food stores were depleted and their only nourishment left was the milk. But the castle servant was not moved. The *fall* must be performed within three days. You can cry all you want, but the law is the law.

Period. With sand sprinkled over it.

Her mother could still spin in the evenings, but she had to work in the stables during the day. She grew quiet, as if she had lost the strength even to lament and complain. Her face was gray, but her body became visibly rounder, appearing strangely to thrive.

In early March she stayed in bed one morning with cramping in her belly, and Anna was sent to Salez to fetch her older sister. Katharina immediately called for their cousin, a midwife in Werdenberg, who was visiting relatives in Sennwald.

When Anna came home from school that afternoon, her cousin was putting some linens into a wooden tub filled with water.

There were spots of blood on the linens.

Anna asked in alarm: Is Mother dead now, too?

No, but the little brother you would have had is, her cousin said. Your mother should have carried him longer in her belly, but she was so afflicted with sorrow that your brother decided not to come in to this world and became an angel directly instead.

Anna had not known her mother was expecting a baby.

They were in default on payments for house and stable, so the church parishioners appointed a property manager. There was not much to take: a bed, a chest, some furniture.

After the miscarriage, her mother did not recover well. She sat pale at the spinning wheel. The property manager determined that a farmhand must be hired temporarily. They still had a lot of livestock in the stable that belonged to other farmers, and the parishioners expected the proceeds in the spring. The farmhand, a lad from Toggenburg, received almost no wages at all. Instead he was one more mouth to feed. He sat in her father's chair and fished out the best bits. Because of him they had to buy rye bread from the mill, and every Saturday they had a to pay a bill of many kreuzer there. Anna had to lend a hand in everything; she fed the chickens, mucked out the stalls, helped in the household chores, and she missed entire days in school.

In the winter she had to give up school entirely. She was sad, for she had only learned to read at this point, but not to write.

Write? What for? Her mother asked.

From the pulpit, the pastor read a note from the castle barrister announcing that the cloth from Nördlingen could be picked up on St. Martin's Day. He then read out the names of the poor families who had the right to charity. Every year three hundred ells of cloth were formally distributed: a "gift from kindhearted people." The "Alms Office" in Zurich was responsible for granting this subsidy. In Sennwald, 51 of 161 households were allotted alms.

Anna and Barbara, you must go get the cloth, their mother decided. I'm too weak to walk the long way to Castle Forstegg.

Other parents sent their children, too, preferring not to run the gauntlet to their noble benefactors.

So at midday a troop of children and adolescents started off. The first snow had covered the forest in ribbons of light and dark. This forest was home to the witch's bird, the magpie. The bold ones flapped their arms, hopping down the path as if they were birds, too, and the forest their ancestral home. The more timid ones moved along in the others' wakes. From behind tree trunks the castle appeared with its crenellated top, the old section of the fortress now used by the governor as a granary, the new buildings outspread around it, and the encircling wall and moat.

The forest ended abruptly in front of the castle, as if someone had put a spell on it.

Barbara did not want to go in, hanging reluctantly on Anna's arm.

Anna gave her a push: Don't be silly, come on.

She pulled Barbara down the path and under the cross vault, following the other children to where they now stood crowded together in a herd. They stared in fright at the paintings on the walls, from which men with curious wagon wheels about their throats and Van Dyke beards looked down on them.

The peasant children gathered in the servants' parlor. The governor sat at the oak table with the senior pastor at his side. The guests of honor took places along the walls. There were no chairs for the poor children; they stood pressed up against one another in their scruffy clothes and bareheaded, their caps in their hands. The guests of honor had front row seats to watch the children stare at the bread now being brought out in giant wicker baskets by the governor's wife and her maids.

The governor launched into a speech because duty and custom called for it. He cited heavenly compassion, Holy Martin, and the benevolence of the merciful lords of Zurich together with the laudable Alms Office; in the pauses between sentences the impatient shuffling of feet was audible. To give is more blessed than to take, he called out, so as to conclude the speech, and the guests in their armchairs nodded and folded their hands over their rotund torsos, their faces rosy between white wigs and lace jabots.

Then the pastor called each of the poor children under his protection forward. They shyly stepped out from the crowd and approached the oak table where the Nördlingen cloth was measured, snipped, then ripped the rest of the way by hand. The servants' parlor was filled with the dust of three hundred ells of fabric and the stench of stable and miserable lodgings. The governor's wife, who came from an aristocratic family in Zurich, wrinkled her nose.

She left with her maids before the end of the ceremony. After the distribution, everyone went to the dining room. Smoked and baked fish from the governor's stream was served to the Herr Pastor and guests of honor; the peasants each received a piece of bread.

Before the children went home, the pastor from Sax said that it was not proper that so many children had come without their parents, and next year such families would go home empty-handed.

On the return trip the children were more relaxed. Their fear of the castle had been greater than that of the forest. They went in small groups, nibbling the rye bread that had been handed out at the castle. Twilight trickled down between beech trees. The birds must have gone to sleep; there was no a sign of them other than a light whirring sound going through the forest. As a troop of girls approached, one of the boys shot out from behind a tree, hooting like an owl, and the girls scattered, giggling as they recovered from their fright. Then another pair of boys found their courage; one of them reached for Anna's braids, which were thicker and darker than the other girls', while his friend pointed at Anna's chest and cried out in laughter: she's already got some wood stacked in front of the house.

One January night Anna awoke to feel something warm running between her legs. She was dismayed but did not dare look with Barbara sleeping snuggled up against her back.

In the gray of morning, she determined with her finger that it was blood. Immediately she thought of the linens with the blood spots, the busy coming and going of women and their secretive work. As she lay under sheets frozen by her breath, it went through her head with a hot flush: Am I going to have a baby?

When her sister woke up, she pretended to have a stomachache, and stayed lying on the mattress stuffed with leaves, her legs numbly pressed together.

Finally her sister left the room, and Anna called for her mother, who was also dismayed by the blood.

I didn't expect it so early, so soon after your fourteenth birthday. The bleeding will continue to come back regularly, every month. Every woman gets it, said her mother, thinking to comfort her.

Then she passed on the instructions she had been given by her mother: during the period of time when your blood comes, never look into the mirror or else it will become tarnished!

Do not allow cold water to touch you or else your blood will run with such force that it will all run out of you!

During this time, do not touch a pregnant animal!

Do not plant any seeds during this time!

And most important: from now on you are able to conceive a child. Keep men away from your body, for within every male there is both an angel and an animal.

Three months later, Anna was scraping the chicken filth from the ladder in the stable and the farmhand was sitting on a stool milking at Julia's round belly. He suddenly stood up, barred the door from the inside, came up behind Anna, and pressed her against him. She turned and scratched him in the face like a feral cat and shrieked for help. He let her go then and, cursing, pushed open the latch.

She told her mother about it, sobbing. Her mother called for Katharina to come home and discussed it with her.

Anna must go away, they agreed. It was time that she earn her own bread.

Her brother, who was still a farmhand in Meyenfeldt, helped her find her first job on a farm.

12

Pathetic. Look at those yew trees, says Doctor Tschudi.

The captain has snipped them ragged. The trees look utterly wretched.

Is it somehow your responsibility to call for the captain behind my back?

Frau Tschudi shrugs and turns away. She knows to appreciate the infrequent bursts of her husband's temper. Especially because the true cause of his anger is that the captain makes eyes at her.

Anna watches him through the kitchen door. His face, tightened by agitation, has something in it akin to a lion's. She shares his anger; the yew trees are disgracefully ravaged, with great holes in their foliage revealing naked trunks shimmering red like sore flesh among the chopped greenery.

On market day Anna goes to the Steinmüllers' in Abläsch. It's a wonder to see you alone, says Dorothea, standing at the hearth in the kitchen. The Tschudi children positively cling to you. Anna nods. They certainly are affectionate, but they're also undisciplined. And Anna Maria is the most undisciplined of them all.

Dorothea serves mutton brats with garlic and potatoes. Anna praises the food: I can tell you didn't scrimp with the lard. At the Tschudis' I'm not allowed to use much lard at all. And I have to count every bean and every potato. There is hardly ever enough food at the table.

I can't understand how Elsbeth Tschudi can be so stingy, says Dorothea. They are sure to have enough money. As usual in Glarnerland, money found money: the daughter of the rich Councilman Ellmer of Ennenda and the son of Doctor and Counselor Tschudi. For their wedding banquet the counselor got three chamois from the Freiberg Kärpf, taken by natural death...

What's so special about the chamois in the Freiberg Kärpf? Anna asks.

It's a wildlife preserve, the chamois are protected there. They can frolic about on their spiky cliffs, and only the hunters authorized by the government are allowed to shoot them. For the marriage of a citizen, for the Canons' annual dinner, and so on.

Anna laughs.

I don't understand such things.

The chamois are free there, they may leap about in joy and whimsy on the cliffs and become strong and for what? So they can be served with knife and fork? I may have grown up in a territory subject to Zurich, but I understand freedom as something else.

Freedom, oh yes, a free Switzerland, sneers Steinmüller. Is it still a democracy if the most distinguished state offices are auctioned off for the highest price? The highest bidder is the wisest. And the cantonal assembly in our free state of Glarus has long since become a farce. The people do not rule. The Schindlers, Tschudis, Martis, Zwickis, Hausers, Bernolds, Freulers, Heers, and Blumers do; they are the true rulers of the country… Steinmüller angrily pushes his plate aside and jams his pipe in his mouth.

Noise from the Zaunplatz drifts over: it is the livestock market. Farmers have brought their animals down from the Alps in early fall and are now selling a portion of the cattle they put to pasture over summer. From the proceeds they will purchase equipment and winter supplies at the market.

In December the channel through the valley fills with snow.

Anna has to get up in the early morning because the house must be warm when the day begins for her employers. She always puts her right leg out of bed first. Getting out of bed with the left leg is unlucky, left-handed, wrong. With her bare feet on tile, cold creeps up her legs. She pushes open the shutters. Her head tilted back against her neck, she searches the sky above the mountain peaks. A dark streak like rain on an oilcloth is stretched taut over the mountains. The Glärnisch glints pale with its fields of snow. At this hour it is a gravestone, a pyramid of marble. Like the gravestone that was placed over Pastor Danuser, with grieving angels left and right.

The roosters are not crowing yet and the moon is floating away over the Schwammhöhe like an unripe fruit. The night watchman moves through the streets. Here and there a maid is getting up, grasping in the dark after her dress, tucker, and bodice, and shivering from cold. She cannot wash the sleep out of her eyes, the water in the wash basin is frozen. Step by step down the stairs, avoiding the step that squeaks and creaks; nothing is so delicate as the sleep of the upper class.

Waiting bowed over with the burning sliver between numb fingers until the first sparks take hold. Hissing red snakes. Woe betide her if they were to dart into the bedroom and weave a fiery curtain around the masters' double bed…

Once the fire is crackling, she can relax for an hour. The water warms in the copper pot on the hearth. Taking off her bodice, tucker, and blouse, Anna washes herself over the dry sink. She dries herself with a cloth, undoes her braids, and combs her hair, not noticing that the Herr Doctor, who was called out on an emergency, is standing in the doorway watching her. Her rosy body pulsing from warmth, her full, firm breasts, her hair loosed from its binding…

There is a creak and she starts, not knowing if it is just a floorboard or that child who is always showing up at inopportune moments — then she catches a glimpse of the man.

Her face blushes at the thought that he could have been standing there a long time, watching her.

I had to go to a woman in childbirth, he explains. I would be glad for a cup of coffee.

He continues to gaze at her, the Herr Doctor. He assumes this right. Anna was a part of my household, he excuses himself, months later, before the court.

Anna, her clothing pressed to her breasts, meets his gaze. His eyes cringing, uneasy, hidden under heavy lids. She vanquishes him, and taken aback he retreats from the doorway into the dining room.

While the coffee brews, she dresses and pins her braids up high on her head, taming her mane of hair, and pulls her bonnet over it.

Her black snakes of hair.

Curly hair, curly mind — watch out! The devil hides inside, the farmers say.

And: Where there is hair there is lust.

Anna, Frau Tschudi said on the first evening. When you are doing your housekeeping you will always wear a bonnet, as tradition and propriety demand.

Yes, Frau Doctor.

Everyday a scene like this at the breakfast table: take the skin off my milk, Anni!

In a moment, Anna Maria.

No, now! Or I'll turn my cup over!

But you see, I am in the middle of pouring the milk. Heinrich gets a cupful, Susanna gets…

Anna Maria gives her cup a push; the milk slops over the side and spills onto the tablecloth.

You naughty girl!

No, you're the naughty one, dumb, barren Anna!

Well, now you're not getting any more milk.

But you have to give me milk! You're our maid, a very ordinary one, Mother told me. You only pretend to be special.

Fiddlesticks! Anna bursts out. Leave the table!

The girl begins to sob pitifully until her mother comes down from her bedroom and asks what caused the upset.

Anna hit me. Anna Maria puts her hand on her cheek, as if to cool a burning spot there.

Anna! Once and for all: you will not touch the children!

But Frau Doctor, I only….

The rest of the sentence is drowned out by sobs.

Do you understand me, Anna?

But Frau Doctor…
No "buts," Anna.

Though there is conflict by day, the föhn night brings reconciliation. In early March the föhn winds rage, plunging down forcefully from the southerly bank of the Alps into the valley. Jarring, roaring, the föhn wind flies up and down the streets; leaving a fire burning is forbidden under penalty.

At night Anna hears a tapping sound, then the creaking of her chamber door and the padding of little feet over the fir floorboards: Anna, I'm scared. A vicious army is storming through the house. Stini told me about it.

Anna moves over in bed, just a breath away from the girl, who grows limp and heavy in sleep.

But there is one time when she has hardly undressed and the Herr Doctor is standing in her doorway. His face in the candlelight, a flat lunar globe; only his eyes alive, begging. She urges him to leave, softly insisting. I've had enough troubles, I want to have peace, we must not make your wife angry. And the child, Anna Maria, comes almost every night. I think I can hear her already…

When he is gone, she lies awake in the darkness for a long time. Her heart pounds against her ribs, shudders of disappointed sensuality move through her limbs. But her body also says that she must not let herself be taken in again. She refuses to start once more at that game with its ancient rules: the sowing of partial compliments, a quick stroke when the lady of the house has her back turned, touching each other here and there, holding hands. Later, the web of glances, the sweet weakness of becoming progressively more involved with each other. Finally the creaking of her door. The man, bowed with guilt, creeps over to the maid, noticing the shabbiness of the room, one of the exterritorialities in his house prudently neglected by the home's mistress. His missteps are now clear to him, his descent and degeneration, all for the satisfaction of his desires. Feelings of guilt, too, after his quick execution of coitus, feelings that permit no lingering, no affectionate words, only leaving the scene of the crime, the tracks covered, dark sand of night strewn over them.

And the maid lies there. Something has germinated inside of her while her hand timidly moved over her employer's back. People of my sort have a heart, too, and feelings. We're more than a piece of flesh. *Rest in the Lord, and wait patiently for him*, Psalm 37:7. *The Lord is with you day and night. Lord, stay with us, for it will be evening and the day is spent.*

Twice the seed grew.

Lord, lead us not into temptation.

There must not be a third time.

Frau Doctor Tschudi, there has to be a key to my room.

I don't know where it is. Stini did not have one, either.

Herr Doctor Tschudi, may I give you my savings for safekeeping? I do not feel that it is secure in my commode upstairs. I'm sure the children do not mean ill, but they continue to…

Of course. I will keep it for you. How much does it come to, your savings?

Sixteen doubloons.

And how long have you been saving?

Twenty-five years, sir.

Spring air sweeping the garden wall, flirting with the green of the bushes, a day without hardship, its fawning sleekness.

The cinquefoil here, says the Herr Doctor, pointing at the ground with a finger fluttered round by a laced cuff. Anna nods.

She braces her foot against the spade and digs a hole in the lee of the wall, working with her skirt hitched high.

The veronica needs a special spot, the man says. It is used in Glarner tea, which one of my ancestors, the surgeon Alexander Tschudi, invented some sixty years ago. I still use it today, though. If one is skilled in its preparation, a combination of liverwort, hart's tongue fern, and agrimony, it can be sold by Glarner traders all over the world, along with their Schabzieger cheese and slate slabs.

While the man talks of this and that, Anna moves around through the supple air. Scents carry her back to her father's flax field, to the hollyhocks kept by the pastor's wife, and to the medicinal herbs behind the home of Katharina the midwife in Werdenberg.

The watering can, Anna.

He takes it awkwardly between two fingers, with consideration for his cuffs, and sprinkles some water. The drops form a shining trail down Anna's leg; the man stares at the white skin there. Then he looks up and laughs at her.

A whorl of sun gets caught up in her eyes.

His wife pushes aside the curtain. What are you doing together over by the wall?

The crossfire of glances. Deep secrets. And now his hand climbs like a bug up the maid's arm. What a ridiculous fool, as when he asks for satisfaction at night, demanding his part of the marriage bed.

Göldin stands there with her skirt hitched up, a sparkling trail of water on her calf.

She does not want to see any more of this and returns to her embroidery hoop and the colorful threads and needles.

And the rosemary bush, sir?

She holds out the bush given to them by young Steinmüller the private tutor and apothecary.

The Herr Doctor says nothing. A thought is ripening in his mind as he gazes at the billowing blue dress before him, the apron, the spade in her hand.

Now to play the trump card.

The budding familiarity deepens during this hour in the garden.

Anna — his weighty head moves closer — I know why you left the pastor's home in Sennwald.

The gentle curve of his ear, a trap covered in leaves.

The camerarius knows a pastor in the Zurich synod.

How his lips curl as he speaks, as if he is doing violence to the words.

But he's not the one who told me about it, Anna.

Drops of sweat on his skin and its large pores.

It was someone traveling through. He came to my *Stammtisch* in Rössli.

His eyes skulk behind heavy lids.

Noble and blessed Herr Doctor and Judge, by my conscience, I consider it my inexorable duty, with all discretion to inform you — you nourish a snake at the hearth of your honorable home — for the innocence of your children…

Anna stands numb, her hands folded over the handle of the spade.

… do not entrust them to that monster, whose own flesh and blood she—

No, that's not true! Anna exclaims. Oh, sir, sir! It was not my fault, you must believe me! It was a terrible tragedy, by my soul!

She throws her hands up to her face and begins to sob. Satisfied, he takes note of her distress, lets her sniffle and says after a pause, while his finger explores its way up her arm: Of course I believe you, Anna.

She lowers her hands, blinking behind a fog of tears.

You won't tell your wife? If she finds out, I'll have to go. Tomorrow even…

She won't hear it from me. We'll have a secret together, eh, Anna?

His lecherous glance, libidinous agreement.

Promise you won't say anything, she repeats fiercely.

In the upper story someone wrenches open a window.

White cumulus clouds are mirrored in the pane.

Part II

"The magic of existence is monstrous."
(Raúl Gustavo Aguirre)

1

... she served here for some few employers, and did come at last to Judge and Doctor Medicinae Tschudi of the court of nine.

Now like all coquettes of fading beauty, she exhibited the air of humility and piety, and even Lavater, who understands so much of people's faces, would not have seen it in her, that so much evil as she displayed hereafter could be hidden in her feminine heart. Dr. Tschudi is an affluent and esteemed man, very active, polite, genial, officious, though he gets naught from such manner. He is most economical in his household, quite diligent, and tender with his spouse. He is of such good standing among his fellow countrymen that he is a member of the court of nine. His wife is a virtuous woman, a good mother, a valiant housekeeper, with a most innocent air, her noble heart upon her sleeve. In short, a painter who desires to depict the mother of God in an altarpiece should borrow this noble woman's features so that his work might be Good. Among the five living children of this married couple only the two older girls are noticeable as superior. If ever I have wished to describe a work of art, then I do this time. I will jot down for you all the features of the second of these children, a nine-year-old girl... violets and roses bloomed upon her snow-white cheeks, the goddess of joy was enthroned upon her face, every limb of her body was formed in good proportions and every move was skillful. She had a middling intellect as a child, her brain was infertile and only through relentless studiousness spurred on by her ambition, she brought it so far as to not be embarrassed among children her own age. However, she is not an idiot, and has just as much intellect as a feminine soul must have so as not to be a burden on her husband.

These people described here for you now, as well as a brother of the Herr Doctor, a French officer en Semestre, a man without the fear of men, of fully genuine Swiss blood, too noble and too much a soldier to be capable of committing any sort of baseness. These are, dear friend, the people who lived in the Tschudi house so blithely together, as did Adam and Eve of old in Paradise.

(From *Letters to friends and acquaintances on the notorious, so-called witch-business in Glarus* by Heinrich Ludewig Lehmann, candidate for Doctor of Theology in Ulm, Zurich, 1783, published by Johann Caspar Füessly.)

Lehmann did not know Anna; he came to Glarus only after her execution, in June of 1783.

Behind Lehmann's Paradises, the scene changers were sweating. So were the cooks preparing the food for tables laid as if by magic. Strict gardeners kept nature in check with their clippers, paupers cleared away the garbage left by those citizens of Cockagne and in the early morning drowsy maids warmed those Paradises.

The heavenly Paradise, the camerarius had said, in contrast to the earthly Paradise, will one day belong to all people, for so it says in the Bible that in God's eyes all are equal without consideration of rank or name. Lord and servant, maid and lady will all sit together at the heavenly banquet.

I cannot imagine that, says Frau Governor Altmann. If the maids and servants are sitting with us at the table, then who will serve the food? There must always be someone lesser than the others, or else even the lords themselves will have to get dirty at the end.

Maybe the devil is given orders to take over serving in Heaven, the son of Baronet Zwicki interjects and winks at the man sitting next to him at the table.

Frau Altmann ignores his sarcasm and says that indeed a reason for Hell is yet to be revealed. I still do not understand how it could be allowed to exist. Devils, then. They will serve the troops of God's chosen ones at His command.

Such a Paradise, Frau Lieutenant Becker comments, seems to me in a dangerous position, on the lip of a volcano, so to speak, with the heavenly host surrounded by the fires of Hell? Such a Paradise would easily fall into the flames.

Anna stays with the Tschudis for more than a year, and as it is now, it appears as if it will go on, the position for the rest of her life, they are happy with her, and she is happy with her employers, except for such hardships as can happen anywhere.

This was all changed by a dispute, which later came out in a most labyrinthine manner when recounted for the court records. It began: On a Tuesday, Anna Migeli came to her in the kitchen, tugged on her skirt, then she pushed the girl away, and finally Anna Migeli thrice pulled off Anna's cap from behind...

Anna Migeli leaps like a cat on Anna from behind as she is bending down to the hearth fire to push a piece of wood into the embers with the poker, and again, already the third time that day, she pulls the bonnet from Anna's head. Susanna, who is also in the kitchen and sees it happen, cries, oh, Anna Migeli, you impertinent child! But the younger sister turns and sticks her tongue out. Then Anna gives Anna Migeli a small push, *just a nudge.*

The Accused now went up to her bedroom and put her cap back on. At the same time Susanneli told her Frau Mother that Anna Migeli was bothering the Accused. At which point, after Susanneli's statement, her mother hit her, and did nothing to Anna Migeli, and Susanneli came to the Accused in her bedroom and told her that she, Susanneli had been hit by her mama on Anna's account, of which the Accused said that she should not have hit the innocent and let the guilty one go...

Terrible injustice, oh, yes, Susanneli, don't cry. I will tell her, your mother, Frau Doctor, my mistress. Anna fixes her hair while she rails, breathes on her image in the mirror as she speaks, the knitted black brows, the flaring eyes. Then she smacks the dust from her bonnet and twitches the frills in place. The Frau Doctor will have to wait, even if that means that dinner is not going to be on the table on time.

Only after a while Anna goes down the stairs, her skirt rustling. The Frau Doctor waits at the lowest landing. Anna stops directly in front of her, braces her fists left and right on her hips, and fills her chest with air:

Frau Doctor, it strikes me as unfair that...

Let that be my business, Anna.

But you hit the innocent girl, and...

Do not get involved!

… and defended the guilty girl…

One word more, Anna, and you can leave.

Anna, standing tall, her mouth open, stiffens. These threats. Recently the Frau Doctor has dropped them with greater frequency. Perhaps she would like to have it done with, but then she would have to contend with the Herr Doctor.

The words I may not say grow heavier and heavier, Steinmüller! They remain there in my belly with my rage. Like I've swallowed pebbles, stones!

Anna paces the locksmith's parlor that evening with violent steps.

Steinmüller nods and remarks after considering it: You're not the only one, Anni. In Paris they are shutting away those who open their mouths at the wrong time in the Bastille. In Geneva you may not whisper into someone's ear, or people will immediately believe you must be arrested for making fun of the police. In Bern no one may say that Swiss blood was sold for French money. And in Glarus? In Eichen a few years ago Melchior Schuler was questioned by the town officials after he said that the common people were masters only once a year, during the cantonal assembly, but that a time was coming "when there will be many more masters." And Tschudi the surgeon, because he accused the lords of "sparing one another, yet exacting all manner of punishment on the insignificant folk." And the sister of Vögeli the constable, because she said it was "time to go after the rich so we might have done with them."

This is dangerous, so many mouths and bellies filled with unspoken words. The words you swallow come alive, Anna. Chances are they come back out in some form or another. Perhaps we'll still see it, Anna. The words, squeezed in under violent pressure, will fly through the air all on their own.

2

...if she had hit Anna Migeli, perhaps the misfortune would not have occurred, and she would not have done such evil to Anna Migele...

A few days after the conflict in the kitchen, on Tuesday, October 19th, Anna Maria finds a sewing needle in her milk at breakfast. Look, Mama, a pin! She cries and shows her the metal object at the bottom of her cup. Little significance is placed on the matter. But when there is a pin in Anna Maria's cup on Wednesday, Thursday, and Friday as well, the Frau Doctor sends her husband into the kitchen to speak with Anna.

This is a remarkable thing, says the Herr Doctor. Have you suddenly become so inattentive? You are not purposefully allowing the pins to fall into the cup?

And Anna says: You're coming to the wrong person with these accusations. I've done nothing different from what I have always done: divide the coffee and milk in the kitchen into the family members' cups and then bring the cups to the dining room on a tray.

On Saturday Frau Tschudi comes into the kitchen before breakfast, inspects the pot and the milk. She finds nothing suspicious. When Susanna and Anna Maria have emptied their cups, each finds a pin at the bottom.

Anna is called into the dining room. Anna, if this happens one more time, I will bring you before the court!

Good heavens, says Anna, astounded. She looks into the cups and sees the needles inside.

Can you explain to me how the pins came to be there?

You will have to ask someone other than me, Frau Doctor. I wouldn't even know where to get such needles. I have none. I didn't put them in the milk, says Anna and laughs. Yes, she laughed, Frau Tschudi will later report to the court.

Sunday. That damn breakfast! Frau Doctor should prepare it herself!

Anna carefully inspects the pan before going to the hearth. Nothing. And the cups are clean, hanging on their hooks. She takes them down and puts them in a row on the tray, one after the other.

Each member of the family has his or her own cup, and only the girl's cups look the same. Zurich china with flowers and proverbs. Their father brought them home from a trip. Anna well knows that Anna Maria's cup has a small chip in the glaze on the left handle. Last winter the cup fell off the table when she did not want to drink her milk.

Anna pours the milk and coffee. When she brings the tray into the dining room, they are all sitting at the table, gazing at her expectantly. Heinrich, who begins to giggle, is corrected by his mother.

Susanna cries: I do not want to drink my milk, what if there is another…

Be quiet and drink! Frau Tschudi commands.

Anna deliberately continues to bring in other things, busies herself for a long time with the lid of the honey pot, glancing at the children who are drinking their milk under the eyes of their parents.

Is there one in there again? Heinrich asks.

Not today, says the girl and sets down her empty cup. Everyone exhales.

On Sunday at coffee time, when the Frau Doctor has gone to Herr Treasurer Zweifel's to visit his wife in childbed, the children drink their milk alone and Herr Tschudi reads in the next room.

Suddenly Anna Maria begins to cry and calls out: Another one! She fishes a curved needle from her cup and brings it to her father.

Doctor Tschudi puts down his book and goes into the kitchen. Anna, he says, my wife is about to lose her mind.

What am I supposed to do about that? She says and looks him in the eyes. Do you seriously believe me to be that stupid?

He grows silent, concerned.

The testimonies that Frau Tschudi and Anna later give to the Ehren Commission, the committee appointed to investigate and hear testimonies regarding the case, are not in agreement with one another regarding the occurrences of the next day, Monday.

Frau Tschudi testifies to the court that she inspected the milk before it was brought out and found nothing in it, but in a piece of bread which the maid had put in the milk as usual, her daughter found a curved needle.

The deposition of Göldin is as follows:

On Monday morning she, the Accused, prepared the milk again, but served one cup fewer than usual, at which the Frau came into the kitchen to say to her the

Accused that one cup of milk was missing. She the Accused responded that the milk was still in the pan, but she did not want to give it to Anna Migeli, so that they might not again think she put a pin in Anna Migeli's cup; to which the Frau answered: Anna Migeli has already drunk her milk and there was a pin in it again, as well as a curved pin in a chunk of bread.

Whatever the case may be, the fact is that Anna Göldin is dismissed from service by Frau Tschudi on that Monday, October 25th, 1781. Anna leaves immediately, without packing up her belongings, and goes to the home of Rudolf Steinmüller.

You must not let this injustice go unchecked, says Steinmüller. I would hope that even a maid might receive her due here in Glarus.

Provided she is innocent, says Dorothea with a sideways glance at their visitor.

I am innocent, says Anna.

Go directly to the top, Steinmüller reasons. Speak with the chief magistrate. Yes, he, too, is named Tschudi, but I consider him reasonable and just, even if his office came to him by lot. Yes, a petition, oral or written. Can you write? No? Then I will draft the letter for you. It will be discrete. The address is important. Most merciful lords. Or: merciful, just, and honorable lords...

The more formal and praising tone is better, says Dorothea.

Steinmüller nods.

Then moving on. Something like this: With friendly saloutations the aforementioned Anna Göldin reports...

Salutations, not saloutations, Anna interrupts.

Saloutations, Steinmüller insists. In our Glarnish dialect *huus* is the same as the standard written "house." *Muus* is "mouse," so *saluutations* is…

I think I'd rather bring my complaint forward orally, says Anna.

The chief magistrate is skimming a letter from a certain Samuel Wagner of Castle Sargans, governor from Bern, who urgently requests the "stern and merciful lords of Glarus, of high renown and noble birth" to take up reconstruction of the Linth. Its condition in the plains between the Zurichsee and the Walensee has become intolerable. Could not the *Tagsatzung* be convened so the cantons could commission Andreas Lanz from Bern to construct projects that would… then the chief magistrate is notified by a clerk that Anna Göldin is there to see him. Anna Göldin? The name means nothing to him. She is a maid of Judge Tschudi. She claims an injustice has been done her.

The chief magistrate folds the letter and lays it on the French book he borrowed from the Literary Society on the recommendation of Cosmus Heer and began to read last night with growing enthusiasm: Jean-Jacques Rousseau, *Contrat Social.*

A maid in the town hall.

Unusual.

Yet complementary to the idea of democracy.

Yes, please send her in.

He remains seated at his desk and the maid stands. Her overcoat is wet from the rain. She clutches it closed below her breast with her left hand. As it gapes open a bit with a movement, he glimpses her stained serving dress, which smells of fat drippings.

Her set face is red, from either cold or upset.

Please begin, he says.

Anna's gaze sweeps over his clean shoes, his clasped hands resting on his stomach.

Then she takes a breath and begins to speak.

She reports her complaint evenly. They just sent me away, without settling the business with the needles. You must understand, after having served to their satisfaction for a year and six weeks…

The chief magistrate nods.

What you say makes sense.

You should go to the pastor. He is a close relative of Frau Tschudi's; perhaps the camerarius will be able to persuade the Frau Doctor to change her mind, to go over the business once more… If he cannot, you should come back to me.

Anna is afraid of the camerarius.

She sees him before her as he stands on Sundays at the pulpit. Lean, youthful; it is hard to believe he is almost sixty years old. And the gloomy, ornate church.

The two organs take up space and air, one for the Catholics, one for the Protestants. The single church serves both denominations, but they cannot hold their services together.

Images on the wall.

Clouds of incense from the Catholic Mass. The banners hang limp and dusty on the walls. No gusts of wind, no sounds of fighting about them.

The camerarius tries to preach for more than an hour.

The splendid, wasteful unfolding of words.

A peacock showing off his verbosity.

From his pulpit he fills up a cornucopia with proclamations, prophecies, advice, and Bible passages. Such lovely, clever, carefully considered, proper, extensive speech of our praise- and priceworthy Pastor Tschudi.

Righteousness exalteth a nation: but sin is a reproach to any people. King Solomon.

Virtue bringeth prosperity, sin bringeth corruption.

This can be confirmed among individual families of Glarnerland.

Diligence, work, righteousness, activity, and the entrepreneurial spirit all lead to true prosperity sent by God. Religion is logical, virtue is useful.

Steinmüller said to Anna after a sermon: It seems to me that the camerarius is making a colleague of our Lord God, an associate for the upper classes: the Martis, Tschudis, Freulers, and Zwickis.

And of Jesus, even, a failure. Just look at him on his cross.

The next morning it is still raining. It has gotten cold, as it often does around All Soul's Day. Gusts of wind blow over the Kirchenplatz, whirling the faded leaves.

As the housekeeper leads Anna into the study, the camerarius gets up from his seat. They stand a while facing each other, pastor and maid, of similar stature, as if they were pitting themselves against one another.

Not much humility, this Göldin, he thinks. She takes it upon herself to barge in here, though she can bet I have been long informed of the business with the needles.

Elsbeth his niece stood in this very room only this morning, crying at the thought of what might have happened to Anna Migeli, his godchild.

An injustice has been done to me, says the maid.

Oh? The pastor raises his brows.

He makes an involuntary movement toward the bookcase, where he keeps his collected texts, handwritten in a dainty script and with red marginalia. The volumes are bound in heavy leather, with leather straps and edging.

Collections of texts regarding the region, the church, the Tagwen, and the asylum, with a physical description of the canton of Glarus.

Generations, a genealogy or shorter genealogical tables of the Tschudy family.

Histories of Glarus or genealogical tables of the ancient noble family Tschudy of Glarus in three volumes.

Frau Tschudi has… the maid begins.

You dare to claim your employers have treated you unjustly? He cuts her off. I have known every member of this family from childhood, none could possibly be a part of such vile business, as in this farce of serving a pin to harm an innocent child. And you are the only one who could have done this.

So you are hand and glove with the Tschudis? She looks at him, his gray eyes full of contempt and rage.

He keeps his temper with effort and tells her to "pray for good weather," and leave Glarus.

Why? She asks.

At that he grabs his cane and swings it at Anna, driving her out the door.

That afternoon, Anna goes back to the chief magistrate.

The chief magistrate, whose opinion has been changed by a visit from Judge Tschudi, receives her coolly. You were the only one who had anything to do with the milk in the Tschudi house, ergo you must have done the deed. You should follow the pastor's advice and leave Glarus.

But my clothing is still at the Tschudi house. And my savings.

Then you should go there and ask the judge to forgive you.

On Wednesday, Anna rings the door at her employer's. He comes to the door and waits with a reproachful look for a confession and an apology.

I would like to get my clothing and savings.

I don't know if I should give you your clothing. You're so unrepentant.

If I have done something wrong in your house, then I am sorry, she says.

Then he lets her get her clothing and returns the sixteen doubloons to her. He also says that as long as she lives she should "never again commit such an act."

The first snow falls on Thursday. Anna watches it fall through Steinmüller's window; she is sweeping the floor with powerful strokes of the broom. Dorothea has gone shopping. After a while Steinmüller comes from his workshop with the recipe book. There are remarkable recipes and incantations that I wasn't able to show you last time.

To produce gold by artificial means

To instill in feminine souls desires and yearning

To compel special items and stolen things to *return*

To cut a stick for beating others, even from faraway

I could use find a use for that one, says Anna. She laughs and rests her hand on the end of the broomstick. Read it to me, Steinmüller!

Note, when the moon is new on a Tuesday, then go out before sunrise, walk to a stick, which you have previously selected, face the sunrise, and speak these words, Stick, I take you in the name of †††. Take your knife in your hand and speak over and over: Stick, I cut you in the name of †††, that you must obey me as to whom I wish to beat. Afterwards cut the stick in two places, somewhat apart from each other so that you can write these words upon the stick: Abia, obia, sabia. Then lay a jacket on a mole hill, hit the jacket with this stick, and name the person whom you would like to beat. Strike it boldly and thus you will strike that person just as hard as if he were under the stick, and yet is many miles away from the place...

Through the kitchen window, Steinmüller sees his wife coming back from the market, and absconds with his recipe book to his workshop.

As Dorothea unpacks her purchases she tells Anna that the whole village is talking about the story with the pins. In Streiff the butcher's shop on the Zaunplatz, the maid of Trümpy the surgeon said that Anna had given the Tschudi children needles to eat. Streiff's wife responded that she could not believe that, for she knew Anna wasn't an idiot. And then...

Dorothea breaks off in embarrassed silence.

Tell me anyway, urges Anna.

Well... then the widow of Major Zweifel said she'd heard from reliable sources that Anna Göldin had once previously harmed her own flesh and blood, so she could certainly do harm to a stranger's child…

Anna lays down the cleaning rag and walks to the window. The mountains in the distance shimmer blue through a haze of snow. The shadows have overtaken her; she should have gone away from here, even if the business with the pin had never happened.

From a distance she hears Dorothea's voice: How long do you plan to stay? People are beginning to talk about us…

I'll leave early tomorrow.

Wouldn't you rather wait for better weather?

No.

It should only flurry.

It blankets the valley.

Snow cushions and smoothes, but the mountains shake snow off at their steepest inclines. Not a bit remains clinging to the cliffs; the snow slides off of peaks, horns, and precipices.

Last January she had crossed the Spielhof with Anna Maria and Heinrich. The linden trees threw their squat shadows over the snow. Jackdaws flew away and joined the drifting clouds, painting spots of light and shadow on the cliffs.

Suddenly a deafening noise. The air vibrated as if birds were whirring above her with powerful wings.

An avalanche had been set off on the Wiggis, masses of snow that radiated into a powder during the fall and forged a path between the cliffs all the way down to the valley.

She stood still, as if rooted to the spot, her hand pressed to her breast.

Shame on you, you big Anni! Anna Maria called out, once the moment of fright was past. You're so silly. I see an avalanche everyday on my way to school.

Silly Anni! Heinrich echoed.

They entered one of the general stores to buy some silk thread. They were to bring it to Frau Tschudi's seamstress in Ennetbühls. When they came out of the store, Glarus lay in shadow. In winter the sun disappeared behind the Glärnisch at three in the afternoon after following its daily course. The mountain cast its shadow on the village, a gray bell over the houses and streets.

Where did the sun go? Heinrich asked.

To the other side of the world, she said. Where only dreams may venture, she thought.

No one can get around the mountains of Glarnerland, not even the camerarius, who thundered from the pulpit on Sundays:

One generation passeth away, and another generation cometh: but the mountains abide for ever. Ecclesiastes.

With faith one can move mountains.

The mountain ranges supply the irrefutable evidence: No one has yet tried it here.

On Friday, the 29th of October, Anna leaves Glarus.

She gives her savings of sixteen doubloons to Rudolf Steinmüller for safekeeping with the request to send it to her when she calls for it.

3

In a mysterious way, Anna remains in Glarus. Her name hangs in the air inside the shops, in the market, and in the inns. Even for those who hardly noticed Anna, she becomes more and more colorful, of higher profile; remembering how friendly and pleasant Anna had been, a few turn against the Tschudis, for they have long awaited the opportunity. Others speak of the maid with disgust.

Nor does the child let her go.

Her departure is only feigned, as when children play at going on a journey around the world in the meadow. As the girl crouches down on the floor with her dolls, a cold breeze blows about her neck; and in the twilight she sees a pale silhouette where Anna had stood.

Rumors spread that the second-oldest Tschudi child has changed since the maid left; she does not go to school and is hardly ever seen playing outside.

Those privy to the household speak quietly of strange fits.

Yes, sadly it is true, says Frau Tschudi as she pours coffee for Frau Governor Altmann and Frau Lieutenant Becker. Frau Becker moves closer.

She had her first fit on the Saturday before the maid was dismissed. As she was being awakened for school, she began to tremble violently. She had "strange incomprehensible speech," but we were able to make out "help me, there are men who want to beat me to death," and she spoke of one man wearing a white vest, taunting her.

The visiting ladies exchange glances. So it is true. They have brought along a bag of sweets for the sick child, just in case.

Eighteen days have now passed since the first fit, and since then she has fallen again into similar states. She becomes feverish and agitated. For four days she couldn't take anything but liquids.

Pauvre chérie... Frau Becker pulls the bag of sugared almonds out of her handbag.

I won't give her the sugared almonds until evening, Frau Tschudi comments. This morning Anna Migeli had convulsions and spasms. Thank God she calmed down around noon. She had a good appetite for her favorite meal, buttered rice with plum sauce, cooked by the new maid. Now I'm letting her sleep.

Then the door to the parlor opens.

Like an apparition the girl appears in the doorway. She wears a long white nightgown and the hair on her forehead is soaked in sweat.

Frau Becker puts down her coffee cup. As pale as the dead, the outlandish child. Frozen in wonder, she watches as the girl hastily approaches the table, reaches for the bag, and quickly sticks two or three almonds into her mouth.

Her mother scolds her. And sends her back to bed.

That gave me a fright, says the Frau Governor. As the door was opening, I thought Anna was coming in. I am haunted by her. How can anyone do an innocent child so much harm? The child must certainly have swallowed a pin. That must be the cause of her illness. And one hasn't come back out yet?

Frau Tschudi says that none had.

She pours some more coffee and decides to steer the conversation in a more savory direction. Herr Blumer is going to become a baronet. The title will cost a fortune with all of the associated imposts! Besides, everyone will expect the future baronet to throw a banquet such as has never been seen before in Glarus. Ten courses are planned: partridge pastry, wild boar schnitzel, chamois stew…

Then a scream rings through the house.

The women dash upstairs, where the child is lying on her back in bed, her eyes wide and convulsions running through her face and body.

A pin is coming out… she shrieks.

She throws herself on her side and a thin trickle of blood and saliva runs down her bottom lip and chin. She puts her fingers to her mouth and pulls out a needle from between her teeth.

Frau Tschudi runs down the hallway calling for her husband.

The doctor has gone out to a birth in Ennetbühls, the maid tells her. The Frau Doctor wrenches open a window and calls out to Captain Tschudi, who is laying a gravel path in the garden.

He comes and touches the curved needle. Even Frau Becker wants to feel it between her fingers.

The child breathes easier, her relief evident.

From this day on, Anna Maria continues to spit up needles, never more than one at a time, but sometimes three, four, or six in one day. Among them are pins that are already tarnished as well as one the size of a safety pin and two small pieces of iron wire.

The eyewitnesses do not keep this quiet. Captain Tschudi becomes the center of attention in the Inn of the Wild Man and the Golden Adler with the first-hand knowledge he has to share. Everyone speaks of the girl who is "spitting up pins." Although this phenomenon begins a full eighteen days after Göldin left, everyone thinks immediately of the pins in the milk.

Göldin, it is said, has "corrupted" the child.

Why haven't the authorities been notified, so that Göldin might be arrested and made accountable? Perhaps the judge wishes to spare his former maid — she wasn't exactly ugly, was she? Everyone knows how much Doctor Tschudi enjoys reading the book that opens between the knees.

Those who take pleasure in seeing others in pain repeat these comments to Frau Tschudi. In the evenings she remonstrates her husband. It seems to me that the maid is dearer to you than our daughter is.

The Protestant council minutes contain the following entry on November 26th, 1781:

Then the merciful lords were notified of the complaint that Anna Göldin, born in Sennwald, former maid to Herr Doctor and Judge of the Court of Five J. J. Tschudi of Glarus, gave his second-oldest daughter pins in her milk to consume, at various times, and that for several days a total of 11 pieces of pin have come out of this child. Said Göldin is now sojourning in Werdenberg, and the merciful lords judged it most necessary to have this wicked wanton tracked down forthwith and made accountable for this crime. The runner shall be sent to

Werdenberg, equipped with a warrant of apprehension, however without colors, to find this person as is his right duty, and in this case to take her prisoner and bring her to the Town Hall, where further action will be determined.

Steinmüller once said to Anna: The shrewdest and slyest of all disguises is harmlessness.

Taming his dangerousness, training it with effort over the years into a friendly purring housecat, which might at most crackle and give off a few sparks when its fur is stroked.

Playing the old, rather dim-witted man who eats garlic and walks bow-legged through the streets. Posing as an amusing tinkerer, experimenter, artist. Most are willing to accept this disguise, loving nothing more than the clear and obvious: he is this way, she is that way, and that's that. People live their sixty or seventy years carrying out the most banal of activities: feeding, boozing, sleeping, begetting children; they don't want to see the deeper truths, they would rather be blind like moles scrabbling in the light. Anyone who knows more or senses more is suspect. They're afraid that someone like that could leave his God-ordained position in life and shake up the established order of things. And at the same time, this order is not definite. No, it is full of precipices, traps, and potholes.

All his life he tried not to attract attention and now Anna has made him part of the daily gossip. His wife nags him with the complaint that people are pointing their fingers at her, asserting that he and Göldin were collaborators. Nonsense, growls Steinmüller.

But he is worried. He has not told his wife that a letter from Anna came with the request to send the sixteen doubloons to Werdenberg. It was obvious that the letter was intercepted and read by the authorities. In any case the sergeant who had come by to order a grate for one of the windows in the back of the town hall asked him, as if in passing, how he came to be keeping Göldin's money. And later the sergeant took him aside and gave him a quiet warning, so the journeymen could not hear: watch out. Fought together, caught together. You don't want one of the window grates on the town hall to block out your light one day.

Steinmüller sits down that evening in his workshop and writes a letter he assumes will also be intercepted and read.

With friendly saloutations, Anna Göldin.

I recived the long expected lettar; I must tell you quickly, that Hr. Dr. Tshudi's child is a misrable child, and now 40 pins have alredy come out of her with laxitives. I give over the 16 dubloons so the money is out of my hands, so I will not be in danger from it: I am pestered by the athorities; this money will be taken from you if you are arested. I am very vexed, wuried, and have been cost an amount of 2 florins. But I would rather have lost 2 dubloons and had nothing from you. With this mesage I send you the 16 dubloons you gave me. I paid the 2 florins. I also tell you that the above Hr. Doctor is having you sot out. As a noble man I warn you to be careful, that you may not fall to ill fortune; pray to God for forgivness of your sins, be penetent in this time, so that God the Almaity will hear you in your need.

Glaris, Decembur 26, 1781

Neither money nor letter makes it to their destination. Doctor Tschudi learns of the mailing through certain informants. He has a rider sent after the Werdenberg carrier. The rider catches up with the messenger in Walendstadt and takes the money and letter from him.

What right did you have to this private confiscation? Doctor Tschudi will later be asked. I did not keep either money or letter, but sent them both to the authorities, he answers.

4

Winter has broken out in Werdenberg. The small lake is as gray as a fish's fin; the houses below the castle huddle together.

Katharina Göldin is dismayed when she sees Anna coming through the driving snow before her door: disheveled, thoroughly soaked, and frozen. Every time Anna arrived so unexpectedly it boded no good.

Get undressed. I'll give you some dry clothes, she says.

Anna takes off her wet things and hangs them in front of the oven.

Katharina observes her from the side. You've gotten fatter — are you pregnant again?

No, no, Anna fends her off. I have merely gained weight.

Plumpness is supposed to be the fashion, Katharina laughs, relieved. They say that in Paris the women are binding pillows to their behinds and using horsehair to shape their bodices and hips…

The next day Anna must stay in bed with a fever.

The house is quiet. Katharina has gone into town to do her duties as midwife. Her husband is dead, her children gone.

Anna lies there, her head burning, Katharina has put a compress of herbs on her forehead.

Outside the window it is snowing.

Anna walks through the snow of her memories, up and down hills, through the plains of the Linth, back to Glarnerland. As she passes through Mollis, she pauses on the road, a pathway imperiously dictated into a curve by the imposing Zwicki house. Snow falls on her face. There — the parlor window. Melchior liked most to sit next to the tiled stove, that blue mountain with the large painted tiles.

Murkily painted landscapes. Lakes with birds, waterfalls, and pastoral scenes.

There was a couple depicted on Anna's favorite tile.

The woman wore a pleated robe. Greek, Melchior had said. She turned away from the man and went through a countryside full of pruned shrubs, hedges, and gravel paths, leaving him behind. He wore an Allonge wig, a velvet vest with golden braids, britches, and shoes with buckles. He walked along, three steps behind her with a pipe in his hand.

Anna had often looked at the two of them. Looking at how she walked. Looking at how he walked. He walked without going after her. Put the pipe in your mouth, she had thought.

But he did not do so. And she walked on and on. Never looking back. Walked between the pruned shrubbery and hedges. Straight on to where the hills passed into the distance and the land dissolved in a haze…

When Anna is healthy again, Katharina takes her along to assist in the births. Sometimes Katharina is also called to treat the ill who trust her and her herbal salves more than the arts of a doctor. Anna is glad to go along and learn from her cousin.

One evening Katharina comes back from a visit to the castle; the governor's wife fell on the frozen path and complained of pain in her leg. She was hoping for a cure with massage and herbal poultices.

Anna had not wanted to go along.

She wants nothing to do with the wife of a governor of Glarnerland.

Good thing you didn't come along, says Katarina. The governor came to his wife's room and asked me if it was true I was harboring Judge and Doctor Tschudi's maid in my home. In Glarus they've accused her of terrible crimes. What applies in Glarnerland is also valid in its subject territories: You have to leave, Anna Göldin.

Leave. So soon again.

Nowhere to set down roots. Never to be able to say: my bed, my table, my plate, my fork.

You should have married, Anni.

Then you would know where you belonged.

Did no one want you, Anni? Anna Maria had asked once. You are pretty — and kind, too, and she had given her arm a quick squeeze.

Urs. Jakob. Melchior.

How much those names rend.

Urs, who was a servant at the neighboring farm when she was a maid for the gunsmith in Sax.

A dark shock of hair, innocent eyes under a wide forehead.

He had invited her to have some wine with him three times. They went dancing twice. Innocent merrymaking. He had caressed her, spoken loving words: darling, sweetheart.

But one day he had said that he must stop seeing her. He liked her too much to do to her what those godless boys did when they thrust young women into misfortune.

We cannot marry. My servant's wages are hardly enough to feed me alone. Where would we live and farm? We'd become outright beggars.

But there was a little hope: he had an uncle who was childless, and when he died one day, Urs would inherit land and perhaps a farm.

His uncle did him the favor within a year.

He fell from a cherry tree.

But Urs avoided Anna all the same.

A few months later she heard he was marrying a widow reputed to be very ugly, with hair on her teeth. But her father ran a yarn business in the area.

Why? Anna had asked, approaching Urs after the church service.

I admit my bride is not as attractive as you, Anna, but my father told me that reason must prevail in marriage.

Love is a word for the upper class. People like us must cling to the useful.

Useful? Anna thought it over. The old schoolmaster Steinmüller had the children divide animals and plants by their usefulness.

Cows are useful.

Squirrels are not useful.

Are butterflies not useful? Anna Maria asked Anna.

But parsley, that's useful?

Roses are not useful.

No flowers are useful, right, Anna? You can't cook them like vegetables or put them in soup. They're pretty but nothing else.

Love? What does that mean? Frau Zwicki had said. I admit that Anni is a proper person, fair and able and remarkably intelligent for her status. But she is and remains a maid.

Such a thing cannot be done by the Zwickis in these uncertain times.

Practicality before emotion, Melchior.

A Zwicki will never marry a maid.

You mean to say that this will change with the new times? One day the hedge between maid and lord, lady and servant will be torn down?

Such thoughts are dreadful.

All perversity, all, Melchior, comes from the devil.

The new time — it is coming. Melchior had said to Anna.

She does not know what to think of that.

She would like to look into the future with a sort of telescope like the one Melchior used to look up at the stars.

We should have lived one hundred, no, two hundred years later, Anni.

It is dizzying: 1981, 1982.

She thinks about how it will be then. The man on the tile will put the pipe in his mouth. The woman will turn around and stand still.

The shrubs will grow, reaching, searching for their original form. The trees will move out of their rows. The grass will shoot upward, growing for the young bulls.

Man and woman will fall into each other's arms in innocent nakedness.

Lions will emerge from the bushes among hares and doves.

And the words of reason, of practicality, which men use to turn spears against love and women? Old formulas, forgotten, dead.

The next morning Anna walks from Werdenberg to Sax, to her sister Barbara.

Her throat tightens as she stands on the road, looking at the little farmstead on the creek, the roof of the barn sloping under the heavy snow, the wooden shingles mossy above the foundation wall, the banks of the stream where strong, fleshy blades of grass, water avens, and yellow shining globeflowers sprout in summer. A foul stench rises from the stream.

For three years this house was her prison without fence or bars.

She had to stay inside or within the dirt patch between barn and house.

She wades through the snow to the farmyard. Snow and dung mingle together in her tracks.

Barbara opens the door. Her face has become tight, her skin stretched yellow over her nose and cheekbones, but her belly bulges under the apron, as if it has sucked the sap and power from the rest of her body.

Yes, another one, says Barbara. And my oldest is already having children, too.

Anna's brother-in-law comes forward from behind the stove, rubbing sleep from heavy lids.

Barbara had been proud back then when the farm servant had stroked her under her skirt, got her pregnant, and finally wanted to marry.

On her wedding day she gazed at Anna with a superior look in her eye: it might have been you putting on a veil. What are you doing that you're not getting any bites? Or, she had giggled, what are you not doing?

Anna had laughed.

Barbara could have her dumb servant, scarred by childhood smallpox.

In the living room, where the stove keeps it warm and stuffy, she has to explain what is bringing her here in the middle of winter. I can always count on you to cause trouble, says Barbara. You can stay until the day after next. No longer. Perhaps someone is already on the way here after you.

In the early afternoon of the next day they see a stranger coming to the house.

Do you know him? Barbara asks behind the curtain of the kitchen window.

Anna says no, turning pale.

Go to the door while I hide in the next room, she says.

Are you Adrian Göldi's daughter Barbara? The man wants to know.

That I am, what do you want?

I came to warn your sister Anna. Well-intentioned people sent me.

Then Anna, who is listening behind the wall, comes forward into the room. I am Jost Spälti, the man introduces himself. I'm from Netstal. I traveled all night. I came from Glarnerland over the Kerenzerberg mountain to Werdenberg, and there Katharina Göldin sent me on to Sax. I must warn you, Anna. The Glarus authorities sent their runner to Werdenberg to arrest you and bring you to the town hall in Glarus. Luckily their runner is not very fast. He feels the need to sanction every crossroads with a pint, so I beat him here, even though I left Glarnerland later than him.

You must leave immediately. He also advises Anna not to stay overnight with relatives in Sennwald.

Which well-intentioned people sent you, then? Anna asks.

Melchior Zwicki, doctor in Mollis.

5

In Glarus the "corrupted" child's condition worsens. She spits up needles almost daily; along with the convulsions a paralysis develops in her left leg. And there are hours when she appears fully healthy, playing with presents she was given by compassionate and curious visitors.

The strange thing is this: the fits come only during the day. In the night the child sleeps as she did when she was healthy: eight hours of deep sleep, without interruption.

The maid who served in the house years ago, a stodgy, elderly woman with a dragging step and swollen legs, has to change the sheets of the sick bed daily, by order of the Frau Doctor.

The good linens, do you hear Hindschi? The one with the Belgian corners. The bed must always be as white as snow, understand?

Are the chairs ready for the visitors? The women will stay afterwards for tea.

Hindschi nods and shuffles out of the room.

Anna Maria bends over the finger-length dolls, gathers the tiny chairs, lifts an oak leaf blanket, and puts the dolls to bed. That's enough. She pushes away the dollhouse, a gift from the captain. Yes, yes, he made it himself — *très petit* — and so delightful, her mama had called out and clasped her hands before the captain as if the dollhouse were hers.

But everything belongs to Anna Migeli: the books with the copper plates bound in leather, the tin soldier, the little pony with the enamel saddle, the doll with the porcelain head, the bags and tins, the sweets. And today she will get more presents. Her head lolls to one side.

Her mama hurries over and straightens her pillow. Poor, pale Anna Migeli.

When can I play outside again, Mama?

Not long, my poor little one.

The door opens. Rustling clothing sweeps past the bed. Chairs are pulled forward.

Expectant silence, filled with rising and falling whispers ohhowterriblehowdreadfulohhow…

Like long-winged insects gathered over the blanket — ohthepoorinnocentohhow — proboscises and stingers stretched out, they turn their multifaceted eyes, eagerly searching below.

She is breathing irregularly, is she not, Herr Doctor Tschudi? The voice of Frau Paravicini is recognizable by its plaintive, sustained tone.

Is she truly going to have a fit soon? Frau Treasurer Zweifel. She does not have much time. She has to breastfeed her newborn. But she wanted to see the wretched child. All who have seen her with their own eyes will later be surrounded and assailed with questions.

How she moans, the poor thing. *Mon dieu*, such convulsions. The child must withstand such cruelty. Look how she arches her back, a veritable *arc de cercle*, so much so that she is facing backwards. She must be out of her senses, by the rolling of her eyes.

Here comes a pin, the captain promises.

An *habitué*. None has been to the sickroom as often as him. So touching, how much he cares for the child, whispers Frau Paravicini.

Frau Becker makes a face and sighs meaningfully.

The door opens again.

Frau Governor!

What an honor!

You have come at just the right time.

No, she has not spat one out yet.

Please take the armchair at the front, Frau Governor. Then you can see everything.

Frau Paravicini cranes her head, the Frau Governor's bonnet is obstructing her view. It is one of those tall bonnets the latest morals regulations have forbidden by fine. This is merely an incentive for the richest to make a show that they can pay the luxury tax, according to the Zurich periodical, *The Monthly News of Memorable Events*.

The Frau Governor leans her head forward, looking through her spectacles. The one leg is contracted, is that right, Herr Judge?

Tschudi wipes the sweat from his brow, answers harassed: it will break sooner than I can straighten it. Within the space of only two weeks it has shortened three inches.

The child cries out shrilly.

The audience stands, a few approach the bed.

Through squinted lids the child perceives eyes and mouths that lose their shape, blurring, a chamber of horrors of cow's eyes, crooked lips, teeth, contorted necks, strands of blood vessels.

Ah! A…

Is she calling for Anna? The Frau Governor cups her hand behind her ear.

Yes, she is moaning her name. They can hear it clearly. Then sounds issue from the girl; now and then a fragment is comprehensible: You wretch… What did you do?

Murmurs. Outrage.

Anna! Expletives fly through the room. Curses. Anna, that bitch!

Arrest her. Kill her. No mercy.

6

As Spälti is returning to Werdenberg, where he enjoys a lavish dinner at the Weiss Kreuz Inn after completing his mission, Anna is making her way to Sennwald in the opposite direction.

She reaches her sister's home after twilight has fallen. Katharina is dismayed once Anna explains without making excuses that she is fleeing and needs money. She once loaned a bit to Katharina back when the barn roof needed patching. She is not happy to remind her of it.

Katharina begins to scold Anna. Hardly has grass grown over something than you create some new mischief. Where do you plan to spend the night? It is bitterly cold out; the streets are iced over.

I cannot go to anyone in town, Anna says.

Then you must go to the manse.

Anna hesitates. Is Pastor Breitinger still serving?

Katharina nods. But much water has run down the Rhine since then.

Anna is frozen through and exhausted.

She can clearly remember the piercing chime of the clock.

The serving maid who opens the door stands chubby-faced in the bright doorway, swathed in a cloud of warmth and the smell of dinner.

The pastor's wife does not recognize Anna. What, Anna Göldin? It's not possible!

She calls for the pastor. In the weakly-lit hallway he lifts the lamp up to Anna's face. Yes, it's true. It's been twenty years, oh the time! The time!

May I stay here overnight? Anna asks.

The pastor notices her harried expression. Is anything wrong?

There is a runner from Glarus after me. Some stupid business, yes, but not my fault.

Once again not your fault, this sounds like it did then. The pastor raises his shoulders, as if he could protect his birdlike head, grown narrow with age. Nervous, just as he was then, Anna thinks. Cowering as if waiting for the strike to fall, always ready to flee in fright. He exchanges a glance with his wife across the hallway. In God's name, you may stay with us, she says. But only one night, Anna!

Anna is spared seeing the maid's room again. A room in the cellar of the manse is set aside for vagabonds and roaming riff-raff. It has an exit through an outside door in the back of the house, but there is no connection to the other rooms of the house. Too many benevolent hosts have allowed murderers and arsonists into their homes. The mattress is over there, Anna. It is not warm here, but in the morning Tildi will make you coffee. The young serving maid nods. She has come along partly out of curiosity, partly out of interest in Anna, a former maid. Anna is freezing.

So like a crypt, this room.

In her time, bags of potatoes, casks of vinegar, and preserved produce from the pastor's garden were stored here. On the rough walls, icicles twinkle. She blows out the candle, lies down without undressing, and closes her eyes. She sees the young full face of the serving girl before her. Tildi, the Anna of the past.

An inexperienced person who became rather smug over her position at the manse.

It's a position for an experienced serving maid, her sister Barbara had argued then. You won't get it.

Oh, I'll get it, Anna said.

When she introduced herself at the Sennwald manse, it happened that it was at the same time as the castle servant came with barbels from the governor's stream. The governor has no more appetite for fish, and has generously given them to his pastors. Do you know anything about cooking fish? The pastor asked.

Anna said that she had often prepared fish for the gunsmith, even wild varieties that her former employer took as payment from hunters.

Then you may stay and cook the barbels.

She boiled the fish in a broth with white wine and bay leaves and served them with butter and parsley.

The dining room table, covered by a damask cloth, was so long that there would easily be room for six children between the pastor and his wife.

Right away the pastor tucked ravenously into the barbels. His wife, on the other hand, only ate the potatoes. I find water creatures disgusting, she explained. With their vile, slippery bodies, those scales and tails! She seemed to become nauseated by her own description of them. Her kindly face became waxy and her porcelain-blue eyes took on a glassy, distant look.

She feels ill because she is expecting a child, Anna had thought. They certainly don't have any yet.

She had free reign in the kitchen, which seemed clean and well equipped to Anna's eyes at the time. The young wife knew nothing of keeping house; as a child of rich parents in Zurich she had always had servants. The pastor, a man of thirty years, artificially made himself look old. After his morning prayers he powdered his hair and eyebrows, and with a branding iron he curled a finger-length lock over each ear.

A grand seigneur, the people said. From the scholarly Breitinger family. His Sunday sermons are completely over the heads of the parishioners. And he remains true to the governor through thick and thin.

They complained about his salary, about the requisite tithing of goods, and the percentage of common land and alpine pasture. He even had his own mountain vineyard; they were most envious of that. Every household that had its own team of horses had to deliver one cartload of wood to him. The other households paid him two batzen for firewood.

In the mornings he stayed in his office, clothed in a velvet dressing gown, making entries in baptismal and death registries, and reading reports from his colleagues on the income of clergy in the territory of Sax. Joh. Martin Wyss, pastor in Sax, had formulated one such report for the governors:

It is reasonable that one may not easily entrust oneself to the people and should engage with them as little as possible.

They do not like to see their governor and pastor get along with one another for they fear it will be to their disadvantage: their wealth is not great among any of them, but they nourish themselves with the cultivation of their fields; fruits, vegetables, and above all, milk, so they are still rather inclined to pride and arrogance; they do not make professions of courtesy and superior mores, rather from youth they are brought up in and accustomed to the crude…

On afternoons when the weather was good, Pastor Breitinger went outside, preferably to the hut in his vineyard. He had renovated it into a country home, as was the fashion for the hillside vineyards around the Zürichsee. The playful weather vane, always turning toward the wind, could be seen all the way from the village; some decades later, in 1798, rebellious farmers armed with pitchforks and scythes chased the pastor and the governor from of the countryside and destroyed the despised cottage.

The pastor spent entire afternoons at the window of the country home, reading and studying. The rural peace and delightful setting helped him reconcile his circumstance of being outside Zurich in the countryside. His uncle, a professor of Hebrew and Greek at the Collegium Carolinum in Zurich, sent him books, the first odes by Klopstock, for example, whose acquaintance he had made some years previous in the home of Bodmer.

In spite of the interesting new book titles, he favored Greek literature. The poetry of Homer. Whenever he glanced up, he saw the arms of the maid appear among vine leaves, bright spots alternating with a rich green. As she reached up to cut down grapes with the crescent-shaped knife, it was evident in her expression of intense concentration on the simple task that she was unaware he was watching her.

Anna liked to work in the hillside vineyard.

Hard to believe that the stony, steep Sennwald ground could bring forth such lush bunches of grapes. They lay plump and full of warm juice in her hand.

One day she was surprised by a young man while she was working in the vineyard. She had met him at the fair and he had bought her wine in the Adler and danced with her. His name was Jakob Roduner and was apprenticed to a master cabinetmaker.

Oh, you gave me a scare, she said.

He threw his arm around her. She laughed and handed him a grape. He bit into the fruit and said, with the juice in the corners of his mouth: It tastes like sorrel. The grapes in Frümsen are better.

She pretended to be indignant, defending the pastor's vineyard, but he kissed her angry words away and twiddled her tucker.

In the evening the pastor asked his wife if Anna had a beau.

I wouldn't know anything about that.

The pastor did not like the way she responded, with such disinterest, a bleary demeanor, as if she were not sitting next to him at the table, as if she had a veil before her eyes.

She sensed his look and stared out the window.

Once Anna had cleared the plates, his wife burst out with unusual vehemence: I want a baby. I'm bored to death here.

He did not know what to say to that, so he smiled his tight-lipped smile, showing inward-pointing teeth, but the familiar gesture did not soothe her. Anna was coming back in, wreathed in vines, bringing the first grapes.

I took them from the west side of the vineyard, where they ripened first. See? They have a yellowish tinge.

The pastor praised her for her skill.

She remained standing there one moment too long with the bowl in her hand, her eyes shining, her cheeks rosy from her time in the fresh air.

Next to Anna his young wife looked wan and small, child-like; it was as if she deflated in Anna's presence.

How was she to conceive and bear new life when it seemed she did not have enough substance within her to maintain herself?

The doctor had prescribed the usual remedies: an egg yolk with white wine, champagne with escargot, a complete course of blood-letting, and a spa treatment at Schinznach.

Anna was utterly unaware of the pastor's wife's state of mind.

After long years of service, she had gotten used to her employers' wives not always being in good moods. Besides, it looked as if her own story was beginning; so, what did the problems of others concern her?

She went on secret walks with Jakob. After twilight. And in the forest in daylight. We have to keep our relationship secret, said Jakob, because of my master. He is of the same mind as the guild masters in the cities and in Swabia: a journeyman may not be concerned with a woman. If he must marry, then he will become journeyman to a woman. Only a bachelor can become a master. Jakob wanted to become a cabinetmaker and later go to Paris to learn from the *ébénistes* who made consoles and desks inlaid with rare wood.

The pastor has a bureau like that, with a panel that folds down, secret compartments, drawers, and decorated with light flowers on dark wood and dark flowers on light wood. One must have fine hands for that sort of work, Anna remarked.

Well, I have fine hands, don't I? Jakob said and stroked her face, her throat, her cleavage above her bodice.

The forest opened up with the echoes of shadows and patches of moonshine. He pressed her against a tree trunk and kissed her.

We mustn't.

But why?

You are over twenty. You like me, Anna, don't you?

Don't worry. It won't happen.

I'll be careful.

And if it happens anyway?

Then we'll be a couple.

... Anna Göldin, born in the subject territory of Sax, approximately 40 years old, healthy, somewhat educated, yet sensual and sly, went to work for the pastor in her hometown during her younger years, and as a lustful girl, though yet inexperienced in love-making, had the misfortune... (H. L. Lehmann)

The forest, now their haven in daytime and on well-lit nights, with its padding of leaves from the previous year, the mossy hollows, the ponds of woodruff and green curtains of foliage moving in the wind; embraced by coaxing, stroking hands, kissed as the eyes climbed the tree trunks up to the filamented blue.

The first snow fell at the end of October. Too early.

The blanket of snow full of waves, bumps, wretchedly thin, ripped from tendrils of mulberries.

Anna was pregnant.

Jakob did not yet know.

The tension and growth of her breasts, the fluttering in her belly when she got up, the suspension of her monthly cycle. And Jakob knew nothing of it.

She froze in spite of her woolen cape.

Jakob panted warm breath in her ears and pressed warmth into her mouth with his lips.

Between kisses she said:

Jakob?

Yes?

Then silence. Melting snow dripped from the branches.

Without even a word, Jakob knew. A shadow had touched him, his heart skipped a beat.

I'm going to have a baby, Jakob.

He did not say a word. His arms slid from Anna's waist.

Jakob Roduner. Twenty-three years old, a woman's journeyman.

You were lured into the trap, Roduner, of woman's flesh.

Hang your future on the mantle. Jakob, twenty-three years old, bound to Anna the maid. Soon he would have three mouths to feed with shoddy work and side jobs. The desires of the flesh…

And I find more bitter than death the woman, whose heart is snares and nets, and her hands bonds. Ecclesiastes 7.

The body of a woman, a piece of nature, uncontrolled growth with its tumescent form, the rambling opulence, limbs twisting around the man, the hidden caverns, covered traps; many lose their way in this geography like a wanderer in the wilderness.

Often enough the body of a woman with its allure has taken from a man his most prized possession. That is, his sanity, the camerarius said in one of his sermons. It would be better for a man, when he thinks to copulate, to content himself with a domestic, prosaic, unflirtatious being. Even Lavater, a wise man and enlightened by God, cleaved a woman without great charm.

The vile desires of the flesh and sensual frenzies subside, but reason remains.

He lifted his hand, the laced cuff fell back, and the congregation intoned the song of repentance from the Zurich hymnal.

Desires of my flesh
That cause me so much pain.
My flesh and soul,
Tug and rend me on both sides
O! Then begins the quarreling.
Perils of the flesh break through
Those tangled bindings.
Drown me with Your love
And crucify my desire
Along with all evil urges,
For which I by and by
Will die from this world of sin,
After my flesh is corrupted…

7

At tea the Frau Lieutenant Becker asks the maid if she sleeps in the same bed Göldin did.

Heaven forbid, says Hindschi. I would rather walk home every evening at eleven than sleep in the bed of that witch. I only stood once in the doorway for a short time, and I must honestly confess that I had goose bumps up my back as I peered into the room.

She does not add that everything looked tidy up there.

Then she still hasn't been arrested? Frau Colonel Paravicini asks and looks up at the doctor through her panel of eyelashes.

Tschudi bites his lower lip. All of Glarus — Frau Paravicini certainly included — knows that the runner came back with his duties unperformed. He brought back nothing but the news of the successful mission of Jost Spälti. To top it all off, the two runners met up in the Weiss Kreuz Inn in Werdenberg one evening, toasted their brotherhood over a flask of Beerli wine, and laughed at the men who hired them. Spälti then spread the rumor all through Glarnerland that Katharina Göldi confided in him that Anna seemed noticeably fatter to her...

Tschudi has had enough of the women in the sickroom and at the tea table, but worse are the enlightened know-it-alls of Glarus: Chief Magistrate Cosmus Heer and Steinmüller the private tutor. Just the previous evening as Tschudi was sitting down in the Adler to drink his glass of Veltliner, Cosmus Heer called down the table: Medieval things are occurring in your home, Doctor. Did you know that spitting up pins was a symptom of being possessed?

That derisive, enlightened undertone. It comes from the French books they recently began discussing every second Friday in the Literary Society. The camerarius has already complained that his duty of censoring the reading list is being undermined by the rest of the men.

On the ninth of December, Tschudi requests that the council carry out an "earnest intervention." The matter must be expedited, the more so as the rumor is going around that Göldin is pregnant by him. I have to preserve my marriage.

The councilmen listen, one helpless, another with poorly concealed pleasure at his distress. After a long debate they agree to "investigate the case to their highest capacity." Two men are to be sent out with warrants to find and arrest Göldin.

The "corrupted" child is to be examined by the most renowned doctor in Glarus, Doctor Marti. Doctor Zwicki and the midwife Göldin in Werdenberg, among others, will be questioned.

The interviews that take place from the middle of December to the beginning of February bring little new information to light.

Doctor Zwicki apologizes for warning Anna with flimsy excuses. I warned the maid for my Frau Mama's sake. She is deeply grieved by the fate of her former maid.

Katharina Göldin from Werdenberg goes on record thus: Anna changed her clothes in front of me, and I believe, from various symptoms "according to my expertise as midwife," to be able to determine that Anna was pregnant, "for one thing, every time she has looked like this, she was pregnant."

8

Back when Anna got pregnant by Jakob, she walked to Werdenberg from Sennwald. She had no idea what to do but was hopeful Katharina could give her advice and perhaps even help.

After that evening in the forest, Jakob stopped coming to meet her. A few days later a man knocked on the kitchen window of the manse and when she opened the window he asked if she was Anna.

He was Roduner's master.

If Jakob is staying up in your maid's room with you, you'd best be frank about it.

I swear to you he is not there.

He has not come to work since Monday. The master looked away.

And Anna said nothing. Only swallowed.

Suddenly a void appeared, a salty dryness. Two days later she found out from Jakob's brother that Jakob had accepted earnest money and was serving as a soldier in Holland.

Upstairs, downstairs, her hands moved industriously, Anna, hither and thither, no one asking what was going on in her head. It was thinking only one thing: Jakob is gone.

And within her the growth making her body swell. Who says it is a child? It could be a bundle of dreams, a sponge full of swallowed tears.

On the way to Werdenberg, mulling her uncertain expectations that Katharina would determine she was not having a baby, and if so, that she would lose it, for as she had experienced with her mother, nothing thrived under such worry.

While Anna explained about Jakob, Katharina listened with her youngest child on her lap, the diapers drying on the stove. Lie on the bed, Anna. Her cousin prodded her body.

In the fifth or sixth month. You cannot hide it much longer. Speak to the pastor's wife about it before she notices.

So it will really…?

Of course, what did you expect?

Speak of "it." The pastor's wife. The pastor.

She moved the iron, filled with glowing coals, across a lacy silk handkerchief.

No idea how one goes about saying such a thing.

She ironed the Herr Pastor's cravat.

With people of her own class, she could have easily found words that aimed directly at their target and were sturdy and not squeamish, that described in a straightforward manner what had happened between her and Jakob.

But for people of standing, such expressions were not appropriate. They had words at their command that could be printed in books, words that paraphrased, politely describing what one meant, glittering ambiguously.

Copulation. Procreation. Sexual Intercourse.

Not a breath of passion in them.

Yes, up to this point she still believed in all seriousness that fine people knew nothing of carnal desires. Only famers felt the horny, animalistic, dark cravings. The iron moved over the pastor's trousers, the tip crept into the flounces and pressed the lace.

Anna's eyes sought the window.

She was glad the church and manse were on a hill outside the village. In the valley of the Rhine. Water flows on like time, on and on until it pours into the sea in Holland, or so she had heard. No one is able to stop the river. The hours, days, and weeks do not stop either, but flow on.

And still she had not found the right words.

They have taken our words from us, Steinmüller.

Only speechlessness is left to us, keeping silent, and cowering.

Anna's skirt began to billow out.

The tight bodice stood out like a shield, protecting Jakob's child.

She did not want to protect it. She hoped it would disappear, strangled by her worry and washed away. That's what happened to her little brother in Mother's belly after Father died. Child of worry, child of distress, it would be better to become an angel directly. She had never heard of legitimate and illegitimate angels. Pastor Breitinger never mentioned such heavenly distinctions in church, though he took every opportunity to warn everyone of the consequences of extramarital intercourse.

In the church Anna begged God for understanding. Her eyes sought refuge in the angel on the crest in the window; it was a strong, masculine angel, with dark fire in his eyes and a sensual lower lip. It made her angry that the glass painter decided to depict him holding the Sax coat of arms, binding him like an earthly being to serve the lords of Sennwald.

And still she had not found words, though it was far into the Advent season; the sexton lit the candles with a long pole to which he had attached a burning wick. Gilded nuts on silk ribbons swayed in the breeze. The pastor's wife had noticed nothing.

Anna, you must go over and prepare the church for the Christmas service. The sexton is suffering from gout and cannot do the cleaning.

Anna grumbled.

The sexton always manages to shirk his duties. After the holiday services, he goes straight to the tavern, where the liquor is passed around.

But then she toddled off with broom and pail anyway.

The maid is not what she used to be, the Frau Pastor complained. New brooms work well, and old ones go bad! And in the evening she said to the pastor: Anna has it too good here, the food is making her fat, just look at how round she has gotten. She doesn't want to move around and stares about vacantly. I have to call three times before she responds.

Anna knelt on the wooden planks of the church floor, moving the scrubbing brush back and forth with powerful strokes. Sometimes she paused, stretched her torso, and put a hand on her aching back.

Suddenly everything went black.

The brush fell back into the pail, soapy water sloshed out. She could just pull herself over to one of the choir stalls with a backrest and adorned with the crest.

Breathe. Her head resting in the palms of the hands, she heard a woodworm ticking inside the pew. It was snowing outside the church windows, as if the sky were falling to shreds.

She must speak of "it."

Preferably to the pastor. He had always been friendly to her.

He sat at the desk in his room all morning. She was about to knock when someone below in the courtyard gave the bell cord a strong pull. Through the peephole in the crooked mirror next to the window, she saw a rider from the castle, finally bringing the pastor's salary. He had been waiting since Martinmas for the 150 guilder. After all, one did not live on spiritual comfort alone and could appreciate roast veal and a bottle of wine from the Zürichssee. While the pastor went down and signed the letter of transmittal and receipt for Governor Ulrich, Anna looked at the heavy leather-bound book on his desk. The baptismal registry of the parish. Years in Arabian numbers.

Pastor Breitinger's calligraphy in dark India ink. The names of the baptized were neatly inscribed next to those of the parents and godparents.

When everything has run its course, Anna thought, and her throat tightened at the thought, in the near future the name of Jakob's child will be there, with the added text: begotten out of wedlock by… no one would hear from her who the father was. It would be Jakob's master or his journeymen who gave it away.

Jakob's and her child.

A stain on Sennwald parish's sacred baptismal book on which was gracefully inscribed: *Let all things be done decently and in order.* I Corinthians 14:40.

When she thought back, she knew it was this quote that took away her courage to speak with the pastor.

Time moved along.

Anna gave up her search for the right words.

And hoped something would just happen.

She and the pastor's wife set up the wooden manger in the church chancel, unwrapped the baby Jesus from its paper, blew the dust from the little waxen snub nose and the forget-me-not eyes. Frau Pastor placed the holy family at the manger and Anna set up the minor characters from the animal kingdom: ox, ass, and sheep.

"Unto us a child is born, unto us a son is given."

From the pulpit the pastor read the Christmas lesson with a stern face. The pastor's wife sat at the front in the choir stalls, her hands clasped in her lap.

After Epiphany the holy family, the three kings, and the frippery along with the gilded nuts went back into the sacristy chest, nestled in wood shavings.

The Frau Pastor exhaled.

After Candlemas the days became brighter.

The pastor's wife wanted to begin with the house cleaning first thing in February, otherwise they wouldn't be done with it by Easter, with such a large house as this.

Anna, who was to clean the windows, pulled up a chair and, holding onto the backrest, climbed onto it with effort, and stood there in all plumpness. The Frau Pastor, sorting the silver knives in a velvet-lined box nearby, must by now have had a touch of suspicion. She said nothing. Had she scared away her suspicion, accounting for Anna's full figure by blaming the good food and the clothing that covered her like a tent, with its skirts ruffled in back and pleats under the bodice?

Anna did not know how to interpret the obliviousness of the Frau Pastor. Since that morning she had been feeling uneasy. Such a strain in her belly. At intervals something seized together. But it was only February. It cannot be so far along, six weeks early. The string beans at dinner must not have agreed with her.

Again the strain. She staggered on the chair.

Is something wrong, Anna?

Far below, a hazy window and the face of the Frau Pastor. Doubt wavered in her voice.

Stomach pain. It is going away.

Anna passed the back of her hand across her lips. She turned to the window and breathed on the glass to wipe away flyspeck. Again the cramping. This time it seized her more forcefully. She almost fell from the chair.

She climbed down, moaning, and sat down for a short rest.

An uneasy feeling crept over the pastor's wife. The maid's face was ashen. Pearls of sweat appeared on her skin. She briefly considered what the doctor might demand for a visit; he was sure to be unreasonable. In Zurich her parents had called a barber for the servants, but she did not want that dirty mouse catcher in the house.

Certainly not. Anna had overeaten. She noticed a few days ago that the maid was not keeping only to leftovers and always snitched a bit before dinner.

Go on to your room, then!

The contempt in her voice. As if Anna stayed in bed every other day rather than doing her work.

Dinner must be ready on time, the Frau Pastor continued. My husband is returning from Zurich and after his journey he will want pork and red cabbage with chestnuts.

Anna nodded. And trudged upstairs.

Sprawled out on the straw mattress, at the mercy of waves of pain. At first the pauses between bouts of cramping allowed her to gasp for breath, then the interval shortened. Faster. Stronger, more searing, more wrenching. In utter dread, Anna reared back and dug her fingers into the mattress. Cold sweat broke out of her pores.

The next contraction threw her back on the bed.

A lull, she could breathe again.

But a new wave suddenly washed over her, more painful and yet there was the urge to push. She let it happen, pushed with it, and thrust the baby out of her. A slippery being, coated with white tallow, a boy, a tiny little thing, smaller than any she had ever seen in a cradle, wrinkled like an apple in storage. She bit through the umbilical cord.

Katharina had told her how women in the remote areas of the Alps did it, where no doctor or midwife would go.

From the bed she reached for her trunk and took the first thing she found, an old blouse. She ripped it in two and wrapped the baby in the scraps. So freshly thrust into the world, in the cold of the maid's room, it balled up its fists and shrieked. She laid the child on her body, pulled up the blanket, and fell into the sleep of exhaustion.

In the evening, when the Herr Pastor arrived in the stagecoach, there was no light burning in the kitchen. The pastor wants his dinner, his wife called up to Anna.

Finally, when calling came to no avail, she climbed the stairs.

From the doorway, by the light of her lamp, she made out the untidy, blood-smeared bed, the maid asleep with tangled hair, her mouth open.

And the pastor hurried forward with a lamp, leaving a trail of smoke.

Half awake, Anna confessed she had given birth.

The baby?

Here, under the blanket.

His tiny body must have slid down. She threw back the heavy blanket and the lamplight fell on his face.

The child was dead.

9

The members of the Literary Society, eager to debate, meet in the Golden Adler.

I suggest we read Gessner, says Hans-Peter Zwicki, son of the baronet and student of Juris Predentia in Göttingen. Gessner, an exquisite poet, fits into Glarnerland with his descriptions of nature. It is not for nothing that the literate of Glarnerland, among them women, are making pilgrimages to Zurich in an upsurge of enthusiasm for the poet.

As one of the elder members here, I would prefer fewer idyllic texts, says Chief Magistrate Tschudi. Although the men in our illustrious circle have already treated themselves to *Emile* and *Lettres de la montagne*, I would recommend another work by my favorite author, Jean-Jacques Rousseau. I know no more worthy treatment of the ideas of tolerance and enlightenment…

I would decidedly warn you away from this popular scribe, the camerarius excitedly spits out. Such pretensions that one can explain everything naturally, a mania that will not even stop at the Holiest of all: the wounds of Christ. From there it is but one small step to denying the existence of God, as this Voltaire has…

Voltaire is not against God, only against the clerical institution, Cosmus Heer interjects drily.

The camerarius' nostrils quiver. Then he says, maintaining his inner balance with effort, that Bodmer, the Master of Letters in Zürich, considers Rousseau a dangerous, godless man.

A malicious smile appears on Baronet Zwicki's lips. A baronet, a friend to the French. The camerarius despises his wittiness, his gallant skepticism.

Many people in Glarnerland would prefer to look to the natural first, says Cosmus Heer. Something of the esprit of the Encyclopedists wouldn't hurt in that. As usual, the devil will be dragged by the horns into the Göldin business if they can't get any further with natural explanations. At the last meeting of the Helvetic Society, a minister told me of three apparent epileptic fits he is going to write about for *Der teutsche Merkur* that Wieland is publishing in Weimar. The first case was of the daughter of the chimney sweep Jakob Schnebelin in Affoltern am Albis. She was the same age as Anna Maria Tschudi when she began suffering from spasming convulsions and paroxysms. Her parents had attributed the fits to the devil. She was sent to the hospital in Zurich, where two surgical journeymen were able to incite her fits when they offered her money to do so. She was caned and sent home, and since then has remained healthy. In the same village a young serving maid had a similar fit, and a boy in Wölflingen as well.

Then has anyone examined Anna Maria Tschudi's bed and clothing thoroughly? Steinmüller the private tutor and apothecary wants to know.

The camerarius is indignant.

Do you truly consider Doctor and Judge Tschudi to be an idiot? Incapable of differentiating real paralysis and contracture of the foot, real convulsions and spasming seizures from self-induced contortions and simulations? Indeed, I can smell — and the veins in his forehead stand out in his anger — where the fly is in your ointment. Not for nothing are a few of you related through your wives to the Zwickis in Mollis. Have you forgotten the law that relatives must be excluded from court litigations? In any case the Tschudis will side with him…

I am a Tschudi, too, says the chief magistrate calmly. But I am free to have my own opinion, as were the many forefathers of this worthy family. And it is different from yours, Camerarius…

At that the camerarius stands up and walks away. The snowy air blows through the door of the Adler.

And yet it is true, Dorothea says to Steinmüller. My cousin was there. The child spat up hooks, needles, and other sharp objects. She herself caught the child's brown phlegm in a small jar and felt how hard and sharp the pin was…

On the instigation of Judge Tschudi, the council makes a resolution: members of the court who are related to Doctor Zwicki in Mollis must step down. With that the most active opponents are excluded: the former chief magistrate and lawyer, Doctor Cosmus Heer, and the current Chief Magistrate Tschudi.

It's a scandal, this decimation of the council, says Private Tutor and Apothecary Steinmüller. The Protestant Council has become a council of farmers, and the fact that the eloquent Major Bartholome Marti has been made chairman does not make up for it. But it is a comfort that Doctor Marti has been summoned on highest authority to examine the sick child. Doctor Marti, he says with veneration, is certainly the most progressive doctor in the canton of Glarus. Why, what he did with the small pox inoculation was priceless for the wellbeing of all people; he was the first to use a cowpox serum instead of a serum from smallpox victims… Yes, an enlightened, impartial mind. His favorite author? Voltaire, Bayle, Rousseau…

10

Anna plans to leave through the back door at dawn and be on her way after the night in the Sennwald manse's room for vagrants.

But it is not until morning is approaching that she is finally able to get to sleep, sprawled on the mattress. Sleep, a leaden blanket that stifles her breath. She awakens to a voice calling her.

It's five o'clock. There is coffee for you in the kitchen.

While Anna drinks, the pastor's new serving maid silently watches her from the other side of the table.

Do you like your work? Anna asks between gulps. The girl nods. The glow of the candle casts a glimmer of light on the roundness of her cheeks, her full chin. Anna feels a stab of recognition: the playfulness around the corners of her mouth.

I won't be here much longer. My sweetheart is talking of marriage.

Anna has no time to dawdle. She must look to getting on. Please greet the pastor and his wife for me, Tildi. Then the pastor calls to Anna from his office. He is wearing the same dressing gown; it seems to have aged along with him — greasy, faded olive, with sagging pockets. He wants to give her something for the journey. He reaches into the strongbox and hands her a piece of gold.

Anna, he says, I'll pray for you. Misfortune seems to follow you everywhere. Guilt will follow you like a dog once you've allowed it in.

I am innocent.

She furrows her eyebrows and glowers.

The pastor looks at her thoughtfully but remains silent.

Do you know, he says after a pause, that back then I advocated for your innocence? In the Morals Court chaired by the governor and made up of the pastors and the senior judges of the five congregations and the chief magistrate?

Yes, yes, I know. I remember.

She can still hear the words of the long court hearing.

... and as a lustful girl, though yet inexperienced in love-making, had the misfortune of conceiving. She knew to keep her condition so secret, that no one took the slightest note. Finally the time came for her to give birth. She betook herself to her chamber, was by chance missed, sought out and found relieved of her labor. The disarray of her bed caused suspicion — and they found under the mattress a dead child. This incident was dutifully displayed to the reigning Herr Governor and there was strong evidence of intentional murder... (H. L. Lehmann)

The lust of maids, of women in general, the pastor from Salez had said and expelled a deep sorrowful sigh. (No one spoke of the lust of Jakob Roduner — he was nowhere to be found, fighting in Holland.) His clerical neighbor from Sax concurred. This is an epidemic;

everywhere you go there are reports of child murderesses. In southern Germany, in Vaud, in the abbey-principality of St. Gallen, maids are giving birth in rooms, barns, and latrines. They kill their children and shamelessly claim they were stillborn.

There must be some medical indications, said the governor and turned to the doctor from Salez.

Certainly there are, said the doctor. In Göttingen, where I studied, the Swiss scholar Albrecht von Haller dealt with the subject of infanticide in his lectures.

There are women who press on the fontanel with their thumbs. When the skull is opened up, there are visible signs of inflammation and contusions on the dura mater as well as blood in the brain cavity.

Another method is the pin prick. It is hard to find, as the tiny wound is often covered by hair on the child's head.

But if the doctor finds a trace of blood on part of the head that begins in the dura mater and extends into the brain…

I feel ill, said Anna, standing in the defendant's box.

The doctor took no note of her and continued:

Then there is the violent dislocation of the neck vertebrae. In this case examiners will find suggillation on the surface of the neck.

Now to the case of suffocation, the pastor from Salez encouraged.

That is harder… Haller advocated the examination of the lungs, in spite of counterevidence given by Heister and Alberti. Haller taught that the lungs float if a creature has taken a breath but sink down if this never occurs.

I'm going to be sick. Anna clutched the side of the box.

Sit down, said the doctor.

But the governor did not let Anna remain seated, calling for her to speak. So she stood up again in the voluminous dress she had been given to wear while in custody. Over her breasts were damp spots from the milk that was taken every day for the newborn of the schoolteacher's wife. I didn't mean to kill him. I wrapped my baby in cloths so he wouldn't freeze in my cold room, and then I laid him next to me under the blanket...

Anna Göldin's newborn can no longer be examined, the pastor from Salez stated. As far as I know, they buried it with the rest of the unbaptized. At that he threw a reproachful glance at his fellow Minister Breitinger.

Pastor Breitinger stood. I see no reason to doubt Anna's word. He praised her impeccable service, her excellent character.

Even Haller invoked humanity at the end of his lectures, the doctor added in support. He would say these words: "When priests agonize over justice to punish some violation of the law, they should also reasonably consider whether the establishment of laws itself is not comprised of crimes."

... and there was strong evidence of intentional murder: possibly the only thing missing here, too, was a proper examination of the business, perhaps the judge was too soft-hearted to give the death penalty, perhaps it was a fundamental rule for him not to execute child murderesses, in short, she was gently stroked with a cane by the executioner, and confined to her parent's home for six years... (H. L. Lehmann)

It was not easy to convince the governor back then, Pastor Breitinger says and looks at Anna, who stands beside him, ready for her journey.

Then I would have been spared fleeing again, Anna murmurs and glances at the baptismal registry. The pastor notices that her former sweetness has been driven from her face. Her chin is more determined, her hair tangled, her eyes roaming.

First visum et repertum of Dec. 13/24, 1781
Currently the child is situated very wretchedly upon her bed and mostly out of her mind. All of the muscles throughout her entire body are stiff, similar to iron springs, so that not her throat nor her arms nor feet may be bent or moved: the left foot is strangely shortened, so that during and outside of her paroxysms or fits of delirium and frequent convulsions the child can neither walk nor stand. When the fits are over, she complains of pain along her entire left side and the same as the start of her illness. (Doctor Joh. Marti, Glarus)

Medical assessment of this first visum et repertum.
The undersigned, having observed the daughter of Herr D. and J. Tschudi on order of the authorities, presents here an assessment grounded in medical science and experience as to the causes, nature and character of this rare and sad story. Thus the main question appears to be: can these events be attributed to mere natural causes or a so-called magical power? Without dwelling on the varying opinions of scholars, and without being guided by superstition or disbelief, I find that, based on the conditions of this compassion-worthy child, the corpus

delicti, *that is, the pins expelled from the child, and those the maid is avouched to have put in the child's soup before she left the Herr Doctor's house are one and the same. On physical principles a) I will explain how, by dividing the conditions into two classes: I) those that are harmful to the mind, as some frequently cause complete inability to reason as well as fearful imaginings from a disordered power of fantasy, as if she saw the maid before her, and is threatened by her, and then 2) those that pertain to the body, the goutish convulsions, spasmodic stiffening of all limbs, great pain in the body and the spitting of phlegm and blood, which always precede the emitting of pins. The first sort of condition I deduce to the fear and terror the good child must have experienced when she discovered the murderous attempts and intentions of her stewardess, and which in a natural way, what with the horror uttered by her tender parents and others and their eruptions of disgust upon seeing the child, must have been deeply impressed upon the her tender heart.*

The second type of condition is unique and attributable only to the pins as sharp, strong bodies. When suchlike irritate the nerve-rich skin of the stomach and intestines, they can cause the spasmodic binding of nerves including those in all the limbs, and even in the brain. Though I may now support my opinion with the reputations of many writers, I invoke only the familiar book of the renowned Doctor Tissot:

Advice to the People in General; *in which he presents very similar examples of both the consequences of fear and of the bodies that remain stuck in the stomach. Among these he reports on the case of a daughter who swallowed a large number of pins. Concerning the manner in which these pins could have appeared in such great numbers in the child, for the child trembled with every bite and would not take a spoonful without having examined her plate entirely, this is indeed hard to understand, and no one better than the monstrous maid herself will be able to reveal it.* (Glarus, the 13th of Dec., 1871. Doctor Joh. Marti)

Only one night, Anna, the pastor's wife said. Even though it is not our governing canton that is pursuing you, it could still cause trouble for us if the governor becomes aware of it…

All the cantons, as estranged as they are individually, will spread a net together across the entire country when it concerns an insubordinate subject. Fly away little bird, or else you won't escape, you'll soon be hanging in the mesh with the snare pulled tight.

Anna stays on the country roads that run through settlements and along small forests on the banks of the Rhine. The heights and passes are covered in snow.

Because Steinmüller's letter did not make it to Werdenberg, she has only the piece of gold from the pastor in her bag. Worse yet, she cannot understand why the runner was sent after her to chase her down like an animal on account of a few needles in the milk. Certainly Jost Spälti mentioned something about Doctor Tschudi's daughter becoming ill since she left Glarus; but what does that have to do with her or the needles?

From Lake Constance she goes past Rorschach up to St. Gallen, where elegant people pass by in the streets. People turn to face her: every one of them Tschudis and Zwickis, appraising her with their eyes, observing her as if she were a scarecrow with her red face and tangled hair…

Better to remain more secluded, in the hilly backlands. She leaves the city heading west through driving snow; snow-covered hills with farmsteads and trees, always more hills to hide her from view, a landscape made for hiding.

On the advice of a farmer she goes from Herisau in Appenzell to Toggenburg. In Degerschen or Degersheim there is an innkeeper looking for a maid, his name is Jakob Züblin.

Part III

"Before your feet stumble upon the dark mountains."
(Jeremiah. 13: 16)

1

The poor child lay there — out of her mind, struggling feebly with distress and death and its terrible following, and exacting tears of compassion from every visitor. Consider, dear friend, how her parents must have felt, who watched their tenderly loved child struggling with bitter death, without means to help her, full of anxious expectation for how and when this heart-wrenching tragedy would reach its conclusion. That best mother, sunk to the ground in saddest sentiment, her eyes hidden behind a veil of sorrow, deathly pallor upon her countenance, her soul plunging into the fullness of anxious despair, desired to cry and could not, staggering she sank into the arms of her spouse and sought comfort with him, who himself needed comfort... (H. L. Lehmann)

I'm pregnant, she says.

Again, says Tschudi and looked away in remorse.

She angrily pushes back the curtains of their bed with a glance at the Tschudi ancestors framed in gold and hanging on the wall, undisturbed by the people on this side. Her eyes fall on her bonnet and frilled blouse.

While he dresses, she says:

I'm staying in bed this morning.

He nods.

Hindschi does not hear well, so he has to go to her in the kitchen and loudly tell her to bring coffee to the Frau Doctor. Impatient, he turns his back to the maid and looks out the kitchen window. The snow has melted; the gravel path and trees are bare. The captain rearranged the garden according to Frau Tschudi's wishes shortly before the start of winter: the paths look as if they have been dusted with sugar. The yew trees are pruned to spheres, the cedar trees to pyramids.

A miniature Versailles in the shadow of the wall.

With the single-mindedness of a vole their relative worked through the garden and finally he invaded the house. On a daily basis Tschudi encounters the captain in the hallway or the sickroom. He hates the sight of those ears sticking out, those obsequious eyes, that low forehead the captain wrinkles dramatically to indicate his sorrowful thoughts and deep concern for others, whose burdens he carries upon his sturdy shoulders.

None sits more often at the sickbed. No, no chair, I prefer the edge of the bed, we're making a toy together. He speaks with her for entire afternoons, seeking her trust.

When Tschudi once carefully put the question to his wife of whether the captain was neglecting his duties with the town watch, she reacted like a volatile pregnant woman.

Instead of *jaloux*, you should be thankful! The captain has sacrificed himself for the child. He is always there with her when she has her seizures. As a doctor you always have to be taking care of others and making your house calls to bring the money in. At least this way there is a man in the house when the child has a bad spell. And the captain has better nerves for it!

His wife is right about that.

Although his work has accustomed him to suffering, his daughter's seizures have brought him to despair. There is no overcoming the mysterious illness with the means he has at his command: vomitives, laxatives, enemas. He has gone through the literature for similar cases and read from Tissot's *Advice to the People in General*. The doctor from Neuenburg wrote in the chapter on blockages:

A Pin of a middling Size has been discharged by Urine, three Days after it slipt down; and a little Bone has been expelled the same Way, besides Cherry-stones, Plumb-stones, and even one Peach-stone.

One Needle that had been swallowed found its Way out, at the End of four Years, through the Leg; another at the Shoulder.

A Man swallowed a Needle, which pierced through his Stomach, and into his Liver, and ended in a mortal Consumption.

A Girl swallowed down some Pins, which afflicted her with violent Pains for the Space of six Years; at the Expiration of which Term she voided them and recovered. Three Needles being swallowed brought on Cholics, Swoonings and Convulsions for a Year after: and then being voided by Stool, the Patient recovered...

None of the cases appear to Tschudi comparable with what is playing out in his house.

The camerarius. Another habitué.

Every day he enters the sickroom at the fourth hour in the afternoon and inconspicuously sits in his chair at the back of the room, recording in his diary and with graceful handwriting notes on the puzzling illness.

...on the 18th of November three pins were expelled from her mouth. From this day until the 14th of Dec., one, two, ten, thirteen, or at the most seventeen pieces have emerged every day, until the total number rose to 106. In each of these last 14 days she has thrown up only one, and precisely within the same hour in the morning between 8 and 9 o'clock, but never during the night. Two of these were extra large, the others of the large, medium and small variety, curved and straight, white, yellow and black. In the wake of the last there were also 3 yellow hooks of brass. On the 15th and 16th of Dec. the child expelled 3 pieces of curved, bent iron wire. On the 17th of Dec. an iron nail with a broad head and broken tip, followed. On the 19th of Dec. a piece of iron wire as what usually may be found running through a round tile. On the 21st of Dec. again a whole iron nail with a broad round head, and in the following days resolved in a whole swath of yellow seeds, like turnip seeds in shape. All these evacuations took place with the most agonizing pain and most intense convulsions and tremors. The first time occurred with much blood, but each fit was accompanied by much phlegm of bilious and vitriolic color and a most repugnant and strong smell... I have witnessed this horrid scene almost every day, so that I may comfort the most deeply sorrowful parents and commend the severely stricken innocent child to the mercy of God...

The camerarius skims over his writing, squinting in order to see better, then stares off into space.

In the twilight, the pages of the notebook look as if they were gilded. As his eyes move, the letters begin to break out of their lines and dance. He shuts the diary and sits unmoving in the brown of twilight, nauseated by this illness and its odor of evil.

Such impudence to sneak into a Tschudi family as she did!

The impertinence of this maid who obtained entrance into his niece's home, where she made eyes at the man of the house, obvious half-promises. The camerarius showed her the door with his stick, but like Beelzebub she returned with the worst demons, *and the last state of that man is worse than the first.* Matthew 12: 45. No one will be better able to reveal the secret of this illness *than the monstrous maid herself,* Doctor Marti has determined.

And the camerarius now wishes and longs for Anna's presence. Anna, whom he chased from the countryside.

2

Anna wipes the glasses and holds them up to the light. Snowy hillsides glisten out the window.

The calm mornings are her favorite, when the common room is empty, with only the clock ticking inside its coffin-like case. Through the small window the light falls on the tavern table.

Toward evening the room fills with embroiderers, weavers and peasant farmers. Cantankerous voices that quickly rise to excitement whenever the cotton market in St. Gallen or the price of the fine spun löthli yarn is discussed.

Marie!

Anna does not hear, polishing the glasses, thinking to herself.

Marie!

She jumps.

You daydreaming, Marie?

The hoarse voice from the tavern common room is followed by a cough. He is sitting there again, that gaunt man hunkering down next to the stove as if he were freezing. Sometimes he comes in the morning for a glass of red wine while his students sit bent over their slates in the schoolroom. The dust, Marie. It sits in my lungs, you would not believe the dust that letters raise… He coughs and orders a glass of Balgacher wine, hoping to flush out his frustration and boredom. Would you like to sit down with me for a little while?

Sometimes when she's bored, she does him the pleasure. After all, she, too, needs some time to relax. A tavern is a greater burden on a maid than an upper-class home; people track in so much dirt that the floors constantly need cleaning. She could spend every minute scrubbing on her hands and knees, and then there's also the tables that must be scoured with sand, and the wall panels must be cleansed with vinegar water to remove the sticky coating and brought to a silky shine using nut oil.

Are you listening to me, Marie?

Her veiled glance. A schoolmaster is sensitive to the smallest sign of a wandering mind.

I'm listening, she says and does not listen. She lets him spin his schoolmaster yarns and thinks about the past. But she should be concerned with the present.

Here she is called Marie.

She also gave a false last name. There is more that is interchangeable than one might assume. For a maid, in any case.

Never before has it been so clean here, the tavern owner praises her; she has experience cleaning. But she had to get used to serving: the nagging voices of the embroiderers, their way of sitting there with their backs hunched, their arms pressed into the tabletop, heads pulled in as if they expected to be hit. Evening after evening, as if they were still sitting in their embroidery cellars, their mouse holes, while their eyes stitch patterns. Walls and tabletops full of patterns. It is not their fault if the wine goes to their heads after the second glass, making them quick-tempered and violent.

She knows from her father what it means to drink on an empty stomach. Three cows in the stable and ten mouths at the table. It is no different in the nightshift in the embroidery cellar.

Often it seems to her that her father is sitting among the embroiderers, searching in the wine and brandy for his Newfoundland, his Pennsylvania. See the Redskins dancing, Anna. They dance around the fire with plumes of feathers waving on their heads. And her father dances, stamping his feet. He stamps out the mustiness in the kitchen, where the fire smolders in the fireplace and the spinning wheel hums.

Buffoonery, pipe dreams, folly.

Constantly looking into the distance.

Father and you, Anni, you have yet to come back to earth on both feet.

Back to earth in Degerschen. In Züblin's tavern. One's glance, trying to escape spaces down low, steals away through small windows, until the next hill stops it. Up to here and no further. Cower and be humble. Happiness can come one day to Degerschen, too, Anni, not everything has been lost yet. She nods at what the schoolmaster says while her eyes see the Glärnisch over the Toggenburg hills, the afterimage of dreams and memory.

... the unpleasantness of this location stems mostly from the Glärnisch, high, quite naked and at most sparsely dotted with bushes, lying to the west of the town and therefore as early as 2 o'clock in the afternoon it robs the

town the pleasure of benevolent sunshine. However, the nakedness of this monstrous mountain is not utterly without beauty... (J. Caspar Fäsi, *On the Village Glarus,* 1797)

Days that do not brighten in the shadow of the mountain. At three o'clock in the afternoon the sun goes behind the Glärnisch and it grows dark and cool.

You must make me a lamp, now, Captain. For my dollhouse.

The child is sitting up in bed, propped up by cushions. She sets up some doll chairs and covers the palm-sized table. There it is again, the silky voice of the captain:

Anna Migeli, won't you tell me your secret? Everything that you have spit up, the pins, iron wires, hooks, nails, you must have swallowed them once. Not in normal food, you would have noticed that. Did Anna give it to you? All at once? How? Hidden in a cookie?

Banish it, this voice. The one that keeps changing the subject, never ceasing.

Anna Maria shakes her head, her thin hair flying, tangled at her neck in a straw-colored cocoon. The dollhouse sways, chairs fall backward, and plates, forks, and knives slide off the table. Cries of rage.

Someone sitting in a chair at one end of the room makes a movement; the camerarius raises an arm and signals to the captain.

The voice retreats. It only begins anew once the child has grown still and is bending over her dolls again:

Anna must have had someone helping her. Think back! Was it a woman, or was it a man, perhaps a hunchback? If you know something, you'll tell the captain, won't you?

I want a lamp, the child says defiantly. Verena has one in her dollhouse, just like the ones the herdsmen in the Alps have, a piece of tallow with a wick stuck on it.

The captain nods.

Satisfied, the girl sets the table again, pulls the prettiest doll out of her pillow, walks her up to the table for tea, doll leg by doll leg, and trills:

To my kitchen I will go

To cook a tasty fish,

A wee old hunchback awaits me there,

He broke my favorite dish.

Do you hear that? The captain looks with triumph to the camerarius.

At the far end of the room a thin hand raises, the laced cuff shimmers.

So, if you ask me, cousin… Steinmüller the locksmith raises his head to look at the apothecary over saucepans, mortars, and inscribed glass bottles. Almost every day at midday, when the women buying cough remedies are at the cooking pans, he comes looking for this and that — ingredients for his secret recipes — and exchanges news with his cousin.

So, if you ask me, these things did not happen by chance. The worst is yet to come with such and similar spookery. As long as only a few are in charge of the masses, the others will have their mouths shut, and the devil will continue to weave his evil web.

It is not only a matter of peristaltic convulsions in the intestines. No, there is stabbing, pinching and twitching in other places, too. Sticks float in midair, needles fly through the room, the child has ringing in her ears, she hears voices…

3

Fresh air streams in as Anna cleans the windows of the tavern. In the dazzling February light, the schoolmaster appears even paler sitting next to the stove. Damaged teeth appear in his wide open mouth as he complains.

My wife coughs even more than I do. She is just skin and bones now; she won't last much longer.

I earned 34 guilder and 24 kreuzer for the '81-'82 school year, believe it or not.

Anna moves with energetic strokes over the windowpane. February light. That defiant blue over the summits, still snow-covered. How it beckons, how it promises.

Winter is over, Anni, the worst is past. It is time you send for your trunk with the taffeta skirt and lacy blouse with the standing collar from the St. Gallus market in Glarus.

She climbs down from the chair and approaches the schoolmaster.

Can you write a letter for me? I would gladly pay you with a glass of Veltliner wine for your service.

Yes, yes, it is fine with me. I often write letters for people. The students will keep busy. If they get too loud, my wife will see to their correction. Does Züblin have paper and ink? I always carry my goosequill with me.

The trunk, Steinmüller.

My entire life, it is always in the wrong place. Always having to send for it, from here to there.

If only I had brought it with me just this once…

The schoolmaster coughs, dips the quill in the ink. The white page seems to wither under his breath.

"My brown and black trunk where it sits in your attic…"

The quill tip races over the page, draws curves, turns flourishes, comes to rest in a slash. It tangles, enmeshes, and extricates itself from the serpentine shape.

You have lovely handwriting, Schoolmaster.

He smiles, flattered.

"… and please send the aforementioned urgently and as soon as possible…"

Always having to depend on writers she does not know. Only half a year more of schooling, and she would have learned the art. She had grasped the reading of letters back then in Sennwald; every child took home a different book to learn. She learned from the Psalm book: The Lord is my shepherd, He maketh me to lie down in green pastures: the teacher tapped with a Spanish reed. Anni's braids bounced up and down to the beat of the recitation; under the desk her feet bobbed along. Now and then her left foot swept over her right one, where frostbite was making the knuckles above her toes itch. The singsong of the syllables. She glided along the syllabic storm, out the schoolroom, along the ten lines that constituted reading for her and all the other students.

Good. That's enough, Anna.

Returning to the present, she set the book down.

It was not until the day after next that she was back in front of her teacher, practicing the strict order of the alphabet until she was bored and blinking drowsily. In the warmth of the stove, where coats and shoes were drying, she almost felt sick. The teacher's wife, sitting at the distaff, gave her a nod: very well read, Anna, next year you will learn to write.

But the next year her father was dead and Anna's time at school was over.

At the Zwickis', Melchior's sister, fifteen-year-old Dorothee, had wanted to teach her to write.

Don't grip the pen so tightly.

First the *A*, it is at the beginning of the alphabet and your name.

Up, down. Like that.

Anna ground thick strokes onto the slate. They were still visible after the slate was cleaned with the sponge.

Frau Zwicki put an end to the lessons. What foolery is this, teaching a maid to write? If a maid comes to master the art of writing, she will consider herself too good to serve her masters. Where would we be if the riffraff became as educated as people of standing?

It has been set up by Providence that the mean folk come into the world with less intellect. Perhaps our Anna is an exception. I do not know if that is to her advantage.

Yes, she would have liked to learn to write.

There are as many words as sand in the ocean, Dorothee had assured her, smiling. For Anna had said to her, you know so many words. And I don't know any.

"… and request that you not reveal my current residence…"

And the address? The schoolmaster raises his face and coughs, the page waving in his hands.

Göldin. Katharina Göldin, midwife in Werdenberg.

A relative?

Anna nods.

Göldin, he thinks, a family from Sax. Just yesterday that name came up — in the last page of the *Zürcher Zeitung*. The pastor, who subscribes to the newspaper, sent it to him. An *Avertissement*. A maid was sought, a maid who had gotten into some sort of trouble in Glarnerland. Her name was Anna Göldin.

But this one's name is Marie.

And for the signature at the bottom?

A… No, none.

That is unusual.

She waves it off. He knows my name.

Do you know the most recent Göldi business?

David Marti, owner of the Alder, sits down at the Friday table of the Literary Society. Since the camerarius left the illustrious circle, they can now speak openly.

The girl has revealed the secret of the needles. I know this from someone who witnessed it firsthand. Captain Tschudi.

The child suddenly began to shiver and cough, then pointed at the ceiling and said: "You wretched creature! I never hurt you, and I still know something."

On the captain's urging to speak further, the girl shrieked and finally spat out that she was not allowed to say anything or else she would be hit again. By whom? She wouldn't say. Then it was out with her story, which she later repeated without variation for the *Ehren Commission*. He had gotten a copy of it from the Court Scribe Marti: *On a Sunday during the day Rud. Steinmüller from Abläsch was in the maid's chamber, sitting next to Anna on the bed and there was someone creeping around on the floor who had neither arm nor leg. Then Anna took from a small pot a candied sweet and gave it to her, which she had to eat in that chamber, and Anna said she should not tell her father and mother. There was also a salve in the pot. Rudeli Steinmüller and the thing crawling on the floor did nothing. Her father and mother were not at home.*

The tavern owner looks in triumph around the table. Awkward silence.

Baronet Zwicki leans over to whisper to Herr Blumer the factory owner, so, we've elevated ourselves with enlightened thoughts, reading Rousseau and Bayle. And now here we are — suddenly in the Middle Ages again with the Prince of Darkness.

Outside the closed shutters of the Adler, the föhn wind rages. It shakes the shingles, and the sign over the tavern squeals.

The uncanny. It is almost tangible.

They chased the half-shadows and the dubious out of the resplendent center of Europe, out of the illuminated minds and open, bright buildings with geometrically arranged gardens. A great exodus of devils, spirits, monsters, witches, abominations of nature, practitioners of harmful magic, and changelings. And now they were finding refuge in the shadows of mountains and the corners of valleys.

Fight against it with the weapons of reason, thinks the baronet, and sweep Glarus clean. With the whirlwind that is coming from France, if necessary.

He shakes his head as if he were chasing off a bad dream and curls his delicate lips, then says: So did the treat contain the *materia peccans*, the germ, in a sense, that was later thrown up as needles, nails, and wire? Who is going to believe this in a time when reason is elsewhere celebrating its greatest triumphs?

Cosmus Heer nods in approval. As much as I understand of the structure of the stomach and all of the connected vessels, it is an impossibility of nature for a child to have swallowed all those things and kept them within her body for a few days or weeks and then finally to have expelled them again without choking.

The baronet smiles maliciously: will this business be revealed in the end to have been a subtle and quite artificially contrived fraud?

A quarter ounce of prepared tartar, Cousin Apothecary. Dorothca has caught a cold. And a tin of theriac, please. Marti the butcher's wife's knee is better. Did you get Jesuit's bark again? Two ounces, as always.

They've still found no trace of Anna.

That's for the best, Cousin Private Tutor and Apothecary! They would just hang her in the end, and nothing would change. No one sees the true causes of these ills. Words are getting sharper day by day, pointed against those who speak out, they bore into ears, gouge through mouths and into nasal cavities. They pinch and stick, afflicting the intestines and becoming the instruments of torture.

The locksmith steps closer to the counter.

Is it true, Cousin, that in Paris they have collected every word in a giant dictionary complete with their enlightenment, and that it gives information on questions of philosophy, religion, politics, and the sciences? They say that twenty-eight volumes are already available, and the collection is called an encyclopedia. Would you believe that they are going to share their words complete with their enlightenment with all the people?

He knew it immediately: it is Marie.

Everything fits. The schoolmaster cannot understand why they treated him so scornfully in Glarus's town hall. Doctor Tschudi did not even invite him for a drink. They just left him standing there. And finally pressed the hundred kroner into his hand.

And he spent two days on this unending trek, up and down hill, through the cold, on rough paths. No, no fluttering of the heart, no upsurge of compassion for Marie.

At the inn in Ricken, where he has stopped for some soup, he reads through the notice once more.

The honorable council of Glarus, of Protestant religion, offers one hundred kroner herewith to that one who discovers Anna Göldin, described below, and delivers her up to justice; so, too, are all high and higher authorities and their subordinate officials beseeched to lend all possible aid to the arrest of this person; particularly as she has done here a monstrous deed, committed by means of secret and almost incomprehensible means the production of many pins and other objects against an innocent eight-year-old child.

Anna Goeldin, from the town of Sennwald, belonging to the Governorship of Hohensax and Forstek, territory of Zurich, approximately 40 years old, fat and large bodied, full and ruddy faced, with black hair and eyebrows, has gray, rather unhealthy eyes, which are mostly reddened, her appearance is gloomy, and she speaks in her Sennwald dialect, wears a dress of the latest colors, one blue skirt and one with hatching, also a blue bodice with laces or ties, a damask gray vest, white castor stockings, a black cap with a white bonnet under it, and a black silk bettli around her throat.

Dated: January 25, 1782.

Chancellery of Glarus of Protestant religion.

He had folded up the page with the notice on it and carried it over snowy hills in his breast pocket as if it were a priceless item. Now he smoothes it flat with the back of his hand as he spoons his soup. And on the opposite side of the arrest warrant, on which some broth drips, he reads with interest:

Paris, February 9. During the latest celebrations the queen was truly dazzling. The worth of her jewelry was unestimable. The king, too, sparkled with costly gems. On the 21st the queen, accompanied by the Mesdames Elisabeth and Adelaide of France, the Princess of Bourbon Condé and the Princess of Lamballe and Chimay all went to Notre Dame and St. Geneviéve, to thank God for the fortuitous birth of the Dauphin…

Almost coughing his soul from his body in Glarus. Twice making the attempt to speak:

The maid… Marie… no, I mean Anna.

Yes, in Degerschen, at Züblin's tavern.

She has not done any bewitching there. Not that I know of, in any case. And hasn't harmed anything. Has made herself useful instead. Züblin says that no one has ever kept the tavern so tidy, and he is stingy with praise.

The schoolmaster's eyes wandered from the man presiding to the faces of the councilors. Portly, rustic heads scrutinized him coldly, almost hostilely; one man in the first row said to his neighbor: Anna is making herself useful there, and here she is nothing but a hassle, so why all this bother?

4

Rough walls and just beyond the barred window is the Glärnisch with its lateral bands and cliff faces as if it has been set into the wall. A part of the jail holding her.

From her straw mattress it looks like a pyramid pushing a wedge into the leaden rigidity of the sky. When she sits up, it fills the window. Loopholes, cracks, lines like those on a forehead where the past is legible.

There you are again, Anna. The valley's gully has sucked you in. On the orders of the merciful lords of Glarus.

We must take you with us, Anni.

Sergeant Blumer, wearing the black and red uniform of the canton, had sheepishly looked away. She knew his plump, good-natured face from Glarus; whenever she went by the town hall, he had exchanged words with her in his affable way.

Then the runner began to jangle the iron shackles. The sergeant jabbed him with an elbow and hissed: leave it, you hear?

The runner, a tall young man, had imagined the arrest of this dangerous woman differently; during the trek from Dicken to Degerschen, trudging through knee-high snow, he had imagined that it would be violent and terrifying, and now finally at their goal he was annoyed by the embarrassing tender-heartedness of his superior.

Anna turned pale. She had been experiencing such moments in her dreams for weeks, while the days, so full of activity, had given her a feeling of invulnerability. She surrendered, calm and composed. I must go up and pack my things. But no heavy luggage, Blumer warned. The way is hard.

She took off her apron and hung it on the hook next to the broom. My trunk, she considered aloud. It came yesterday with the mail. With everything in it, clothing for the warmer seasons…

Züblin can send it after you, Blumer said. And after a pause: if necessary.

Anna gave him a wary glance.

But I won't be imprisoned in Glarus, will I?

You should expect to be held during the investigation, maiden.

Then she said to Züblin: Put the trunk in the attic. I will be back soon.

For two days and part of a night, with hands bound she followed the black and red officer's uniform over heights and snowy summits. The landscape was furrowed, cut by chains of hills and intersecting gullies. In the deep flumes and on ridges of hills the snow was very deep. In Wattwil Blumer came over with a coachman who had agreed to drive them through steep Hummelwald, but the coach got stuck in a bend in the path, and then it had to turn back once the wheels were cleared of snow.

The three continued on foot. The runner complained. The Glarner lords are so stingy, they should have given us a coach to use, then we could have stayed on the valley roads: through the Rhine valley to Sargans, from there through the Walensee channel to Mollis and Glarus. The sergeant agreed. He had asked the council for a coach. They asked, is it the new custom to drive criminals to jail, as if they're nobility? And ordered him to bring the criminal on foot with her hands bound in iron shackles. The maid has cost us a lot; you must not let her escape. We have already spent 800 guilder on Anna for administrative costs, and set 100 kroner on her head.

Lead Anna to Glarus like a circus bear?

It did not make sense to him. She was already stirring up excitement in the villages. Looks, calls: What did the woman do? Is she dangerous? In Wattwil a woman in the crowd had suddenly called out: The runners are wearing the colors of Glarus! This is Göldin, the witch who poisoned a child in Glarus with pins!

They stopped in Ricken before nightfall. The sergeant took off Anna's shackles so she could spoon her soup. Once the worst hunger subsided, she asked:

The people of Glarus want to imprison me for a couple of pins in the milk? Why didn't they do something immediately? Spälti said the little girl became sick. What docs that have to do with me?

Blumer cut off a portion of his ham hock and put it in Anna's soup.

You need your strength, Anni. He said nothing more.

In the early morning they went on. Drifts of snow covered the road. Snow got into Anna's shoes; the top layers of leather over the toes had come loose.

Her toes were red from cold. They began to itch and finally to bleed.

The sergeant tore up a handkerchief and wrapped her feet with the rags.

Further and further through hazy white.

A winter sun that made one freeze and hurt the eyes.

In Kaltbrunn, where they stopped again, the wine loosened the runner's tongue.

I never imagined it would be so easy.

In Glarus they drilled it into my head that arresting a witch is dangerous. They gave me good advice for the road: don't touch her. You wouldn't be the first man to get caught in her web.

In the Linth valley a harsh wind blew, and Anna held her thin shawl closed as she walked. She felt a stabbing in her throat and tension in her lower body, the recurring need to pass water.

I must go, Blumer.

Again so soon?

No, I can't let you go behind the barn, what if you were to disappear behind those poplars, never to be seen again? Anna, the woman so essential to the town of Glarus? I could just as well quit the service. But the high lords and governors know no pardon. Anna crouched on the side of the path. Puffed up like a crow she squatted under the poplar. Don't look, she commanded as she raised her skirts. Yellow rivulets cut through the snow. The runner watched anyway. She scolded him.

Prudish woman. They will drive such posturing from her. In Gaster a few years ago they cut a witch's tongue out. And fifty years back in a village in Zug they tortured a witch, stretching her with stone weights so she became as thin as blotting paper…

The people of Glarus were feverishly excited over Anna's arrival. Those on Göldin's side feared, as Cosmus Heer put it, a *malheur* that would no longer be so easy to delete from the Glarus history books.

For those on the side of the Tschudis, the fate of the witch was already decided. Judge Tschudi alone did not know whether to wish for or fear Anna's arrival.

She was certainly there already, even without being physically present.

The house was possessed.

Awake and in half-sleep the child saw the maid.

She screamed her name. The sharp *A* penetrated the doors of rooms, the walls of corridors; invisible arrowheads remained stuck in the ears and backs of visitors.

Everything happened in the name of Anna.

Tschudi had sent her from their home, if reluctantly, and now she had returned in a form one hundredfold more powerful, lodged in every nook and cranny.

Never before had a maid exerted so much control over her employers.

Anna was still between them in their marriage bed.

You got her pregnant!

I swear I did not!

Witch's dog!

His wife's accusations that he does nothing for their daughter are contradictory to reality; he has done everything to his best ability and according to the newest advances in medical science. Twice each day he checks her pulse, which oscillates between weak and hard and full.

He examines her face, which will suddenly go pale, then quickly flush, her eyes snapping shut, contorting horridly.

He has prescribed a double bleeding. And administered clysters, vesicants, and, on the advice of a colleague blew tobacco smoke into the child's mouth during her spells, at which she always awoke but fell right back into convulsions. He has heaped oxymel of squill and cream of tartar into her open mouth.

He applied an emollient cataplasm with theriac to her neck, had her feet placed in warm water and rubbed, and prescribed another clyster. On top of that he gave her camphor oil, foetida, antihysterics, and remedy number 15 from the medical journal of Tissot to calm her during the day: *Take of the Flowers of St. John's Wort, of Elder, and of Melilot, of each a few Pinches; put them into the Bottom of an Ewer or Vessel, with half an Ounce of Oil of Turpentine, and fill it up with boiling Water.*

All in vain, says the camerarius to the judge. There is no herb that can fight this, no doctorates from Kassel or Göttingen can quell this evil. We must manage it through another direction entirely. With all discretion, of course. I know a man in Pfaffhausen, not far from Zurich.

When they reached the first houses on the road into town with Anna, Blumer ordered the runner to put the heavy iron shackles on the criminal so as to satisfy the council's orders for the last stretch of road at least.

Soon children were jeering all around her; the news of Anna's arrival ran like wild fire through the streets. Below the front awning of the town hall, where a stretched bearskin hung, a flock of curious people crowded.

It would not have surprised them if Anna had flown over the Wiggis on a broomstick, her hair flying behind her like a fiery beacon, spraying sparks behind it. Or she could have returned in animal form, as a raven, chained and carried in a cage by the officer. The people's fantasy, otherwise drained away through their hard labor, had been inflamed by the unusual events.

Anna finally appeared with slow steps. Only with effort was she able to stay upright between sergeant and runner.

A veritable witch. One woman spat at her. Anna looked up. The baker's wife! What had distorted the familiar face during her absence? Sneering mouth, narrowed eyes, relishing it all.

Anna had seen such faces before. Back then in Sennwald, when they said she had killed her baby.

... in short, she was gently stroked with a cane by the executioner, and confined to her parent's home for six years...

She had hardly felt the cane strokes.

But their looks burned, the shame of standing half-naked among the onlookers. Lecherous eyes. Whispers.

Where is the executioner whipping her exactly? Can you see?

On her thighs? Her buttocks?

Her shift has turned red! She must be in terrible pain.

It serves her right. After all she let him caress her.

The minister?

No, Roduner. Jakob.

He jilted her, the slut, the disgrace.

He realized what sort of person she was, and just in time.

Sinful, killing the fruit of her womb.

Her own flesh and blood.

And Roduner?

Valiantly fighting the good fight in battle, his parents have received word from him in Holland.

Anna, imprisoned in the top story of the town hall. For days. No interrogations. An uncanny peace. The days leave their traces of shadow and light on the Glärnisch, the times of day can be read on the coloring of the cliffs.

Listening to time trickling by as you sit silently on the edge of the straw mattress.

Sometimes Anna is startled by the sound of thunder. Streams of snow sail down a steep drop and disappear further below between the cliffs, as if the Glärnisch were hollow, as if it devoured and swallowed with some invisible maw.

5

Nothing can be concealed here.

An uncanny place.

Inflated silence.

Every step echoes.

Spy-mirrors mounted at angles on windows flash, reflecting shadowy figures in the rooms above the streets.

Irmiger's visit should remain secret in spite of this. Even the captain admits it. But the livestock doctor from Pfaffhausen, marching against the devil's army, wants to make an impression at all costs.

He arrives in Glarus in a chaise of the newest model and gets out on the Adlerplatz rather than at Doctor Tschudi's. He drapes his cloak and brocade scarf about himself, the gold chain on his breast sparkling like a Bürgermeister's, bends his head topped with its velvet beret and oriental feather plumage, and reads the menu board: soup, appetizers, trout, local game, sausages, cooked plums, tender-shelled almonds, and nut cake.

In the dining room, where first he consumes trout and then a leg of lamb, he loudly announces to the innkeeper that he must fortify himself for the work he still has before him.

The guests, who gather there in large numbers at noon, lower their knives and forks. Doctor Tschudi called me to heal his possessed child. Yes, yes, in complicated cases the arts of physicians soon come to an end, then one with other methods must come — this is a science of its own. I have successfully treated many similar cases in Zurich. There is much to do in this business, all over the country. Devils are on the loose in these bad times, all they need is for one who knows how to call them to step forward, one like this maid, and they are immediately up to mischief — and they have a predilection for innocent children.

He speaks with lively gestures to the other tables, where everyone is listening to him, some in wonder, others in disapproval.

Later many residents of Glarus say that in the Tschudi house Irmiger "drove all the evil creatures to their knees, that is, they fell to their knees in laughter."

He makes them show him the expelled nails. He draws a cross with sigils in white lead on the wall and drills a hole on the threshold and hammers in a nail.

He gives instructions for the house to be fumigated before dawn. He feels the child's body and announces that there are many objects inside that must be driven out and that he will administer a remedy. He gives orders for freshly spat pins and nails to be deposited in an open grave in the cemetery, and in the absence of an open grave, they must be washed under running water.

Irmiger also confirms the suspicion that has already spread through town: that the pins and nails grew within the child out of the treat. He resents the ridicule of the enlightened folk. One year later, when he is attempting to cure a nail-spitting boy with the same methods, he writes the following text, which is published in Rahn's medical journal *Gazette de santé* in 1783 in Zurich: *O, the naïve farmers, how they will unlock their maws and noses over these things that do not occur every day, whereas they have not the slightest idea of what is happening every day, though it is often more shocking and inexplicable! Take this nail, which you see there. It arose out of flesh and blood. This is a wonder, for it is only a simple nail: but look at the baby, how it grows in its mother's body, made up of so many thousands of veins and nerves, and born into the world also a wonder, yet you cannot comprehend how a nail could grow and be expelled from a body, in the same manner as a child is built and born.*

Irmiger gives the child tea to drink, the leaves of which are inscribed with the words: Help, Lord Jesus! He pesters her with vomitives, laxatives, and enemas, and still the devil does not yield. But no more needles come out and her foot still will not straighten even after he applies his poultices. Finally he says: there is nothing more to be done. No one else can help her but that person who corrupted the child…

He takes a few Louis d'or as payment and climbs back into his coach.

Do you know what Irmiger said, Cousin Tutor and Apothecary?

The times are bad, the devil is on the loose.

Then I realized: God is never on the loose, unfortunately.

He had only just begun to go about freely when they nailed His hands and feet to the cross, hung Him on the family altar, suspended Him in golden shrines, and closed Him up in the pages of their yellowed hymnals, Bibles, and catechisms. The devil on the loose is sure to cause them fewer problems than God on the loose would, Cousin.

Anna was arrested three weeks ago.

And still she does not know why she is being held. What's going on, Blumer? She asks when he brings her food from the officers' barracks.

There is a special matter that's been brought up, he explains. In Glarus there is a Protestant, a Catholic, and a common jurisdiction, and they are arguing over which forum should try you. The Tschudis are for the Protestant court. Their opponents are for the common court, because they claim that the Protestant council has been depleted of their best minds, since the relatives of Doctor Zwicki in Mollis were dismissed… it's a court of farmers who say yes and nod Amen to everything Tschudi says.

Anna does not understand.

This whirlwind on her account.

It is calm in the middle of the whirlwind. There she must sit and wait between damp walls.

This inactivity, Steinmüller.

I've been busy my entire life.

Moving here, moving there, away from the shadows. Now the shadows have overtaken me and grow inside me.

I've been thinking, Steinmüller.

I speak with you even though you can't hear me where you are in Abläsch. Or are you in the neighboring cell after all? Blumer said that Anna Maria Tschudi incriminated you with certain statements. I have laughed at your inclination for philosophizing, but now I, too, am thinking: where have I been, where am I going, and why?

The mountains are there so that my eyes might never meet empty space.

The first confinement, back then in Sennwald, was quite different from this. "Confined to her parent's home," Lehmann had written, but her parents were long dead and the house sold. She was imprisoned in the home of her youngest sister Barbara, who was born nine years after her, in August 1743 and married to Adrian Appenzeller in Sax.

Anna had to earn her keep with spinning, according to the court's decision.

She was not allowed to leave their home. The patch of dirt between house and barn marked the boundary of her prison. When parents went out to work in the fields, they left their children in the care of the "child murderess." The children were attached to the silent, black-haired woman, who combed cotton yarn and spun finest löthli yarn late into the night. A skein is still only worth two kreuzer at the market, her brother-in-law said when she reached for a second potato at supper.

She hated his face, disfigured by pox marks, and his sallow, lashless eyes.

He watched her every move.

If there were no night to bring an end to day, then the days, each so similar to the next, would have merged into one.

Her body hunched up from cold on the mattress. All it was really was a stuffed sack that smelled of decay and the potatoes it had previously contained. The sheets froze from her breath. No warm corner, no warm wall.

Her brother-in-law was asleep not far away. She could hear him snuffling like an animal.

This narrow world in which she created a no man's land for herself between waking and dreaming. In this hour her body threw no shadow; it could pass through the walls.

Walking the tightrope on the seams between days.

She lost any feeling for the passage of time. Seasons came and went but it seemed to Anna as if it were always winter in Sax.

Once Pastor Breitinger wrote her a letter: "Be virtuous, behave at home, pray, and do your work." Below he added a couple of uplifting passages from a book. He never came by even though it was only a short trip from Sennwald to Sax by coach.

On the evening of the new moon in March, her brother-in-law borrowed an axe from a neighbor and, swinging it casually, walked up to Anna in the stable. She yelped and he gloated over her surprise. Take this rope. You've got to drag a pig out onto the dirt. I'm going to slaughter it. He orders her to stand there with a bucket to catch the light red fountain that shot out after the artery was severed.

Face and apron were sprayed red.

You've got the measles, her brother-in-law teased her.

Anna became upset.

She rebelled when he brought out a second pig to slaughter. I can't do this again. He called for Barbara, but she refused to help him and exploded at Anna: Do you think you're too good for this miserable work, you whore?

In the evening the sky over the Kreuzberg mountain turned red, as if the pigs' blood had gathered there, too.

Red skies bring evil times, the people in the village said. Other signs followed that spring: earthquakes, a comet, bad weather, malformed babies born, and flooding.

In the third year of her imprisonment, when the snow was melting, Anna stood at the window and felt the tremors of the earth. During quiet times it had gathered its strength in secret chambers.

At night, Anna worked out a plan to escape. One cloudy, moonless night, she walked to Werdenberg to her cousin Katharina. No one went after her; her brother-in-law was happy that she was gone and the authorities in Forstegg had long had more important things to do than track down a maid.

6

Göldin is imprisoned in the town hall. She is fed, she has peace. And all this time our daughter is suffering from torments, and I suffer with her, Frau Tschudi reproaches her husband in front of the camerarius.

What is everyone waiting for?

What you're saying upsets me, too, the judge responds. This unending debate in the council over which court will deal with the case!

A cabal of opponents, I'm sure.

The camerarius agrees with him. In December the Catholic court weaseled out of the business with convoluted explanations, and now in their resolution of February 25th they've made an about-face, declaring themselves ready to take part "as proof of friendly mutual understanding and also for a number of reasons"! It is clear to me what's going on. Göldin's supporters have worked on the Catholics so as to bring the trial before the common court at all costs!

I know a way to make the council get a move on, says Tschudi. He then suggests the somewhat archaic, yet still applicable Law of Fifty…

On March 2nd, shortly before noon, Steinmüller enters the apothecary and waits, pacing across the concrete tiles dappled with sunlight, until Herr Surgeon Blumer's maid has finally bought her wild poppy syrup, three ounces of sulfur, a pinch of Virginia snake-root, and a quarter ounce of camphor oil.

Once the door closes behind her, the locksmith starts off: Cousin, you should have witnessed that spectacle!

Yesterday I was summoned before the council to account for the letter I wrote Anna.

Yes, how ridiculous.

Because of certain dark parts, they are considering this text to be a dangerous document, as they put it. As if there were anything but dark parts in their Göldin business! In any case my letter is considered of dubious intent, the only tangible thing they have. They turn it around and flip it over, trying to find meaning in it like a Bible scholar. I was just about to open my mouth to give my explanation, when I heard a great commotion. Men were pushing past the sergeant into the council chambers, one after the other, until there were fifty in total led by Judge and Doctor Tschudi, with the captain on his heels.

I looked into their faces and saw nothing but Tschudi relatives, Tschudis as far as I could see, from Glarus and the other valley communities. There were even farmers from Kleintal that Tschudi had previously lent money to. As they say, the borrower is the lender's servant. All fifty arranged themselves before the gracious lords of the council. Fifty Tschudis against sixty councilmen!

Then the chairman Bartholome Marti asked in fury:

What is meant by this deployment of men?

At that Judge Tschudi said: With this "respectful showing" — yes, that's what he said, Cousin! — he demanded that the Göldi business be immediately brought before the Protestant court. It belongs there because Göldin was a part of his household during the time that she committed the crime. Failing this, he must remind them of the extraordinary law yet still applicable, in which fifty valiant, honorable men had the right to demand a convening of the citizens of the community. In this case the high lords must hear the opinion of the people as to which court the business belongs!

The "respectful showing" made an impression, Cousin! The council decided ad hoc to begin the hearing in the Protestant council chambers immediately. The treasurer Jost Heiz and Governor Altmann of Ennenda were named the examiners, and the proceedings will be recorded by Canton Scribe Kubli Netstal.

Fifty Tschudis against one maid!

Second visum reperatum from the 10th-21st of March, 1782:

The three men ordered here by the authorities, accompanied by their officers, met the little girl while she lay in an armchair and in her right mind, so that she entertained herself with her childish games where she lay, and answered everything reasonably. At times however during the five-hour-long presence of the Ehren Commission, she was beset with many fits of convulsions and bewilderment of the senses lasting hardly two minutes, in which the child suddenly became senseless, turning quite red within an instant, her pulse quickened, beating hard and full, and the muscles about her mouth trembled. Then she stretched out her right foot, wound her arms around, moaned, was quiet again, and then complained of terrible pain in her left foot and head. Another strange aspect of this unusual phenomenon encountered was the child's frequent need to have a bowel movement or pass water. Thereupon, she turned pale, her pulse slowed down as quickly as lightening, and almost collapsed before she did finally pass out, but she soon returned to her mind. She has utterly lost the former convulsive tension in all her muscles, and it appears to have moved to the left foot alone, which is now utterly useless, painful and contracted against her body, so that if forced it would sooner break than bend. The attempts made have caused in the child convulsive fits and great pain each time, on which account the child must live her life so wretchedly in the one place. Incidentally, she can sleep, and often eats with an appetite, so that she continues to remain rather healthy in body."(Johann Marti, M.D.)

7

The smaller Anna appears on her sack of straw, forgotten in the shadow of the Glärnisch, the more powerful she grows in the minds of the people. She grows larger and larger and swells into a monster, a giant, a sorceress with dangerous powers.

The morning of March 10th contributes to this.

In the council chambers, three stories below Anna where she sits on her sack of straw, the *visum et reperatum* is read aloud by the scribe. Doctor Marti then enters and answers the popular question of whether he considers Anna Maria's illness to be the work of the devil. He has drawn up his opinion in a letter to a friend in Zurich:

I would almost admit that the so-called Prince of Darkness is much too powerful to have to do with suchlike children's games: but I can never believe this, that between St. Michael above and Satan below such astounding chasms should be empty. Is it not possible that even in this great space between, ghostly creatures swarm unseen by us, and that they may work with a free will and can be good or evil, and so possibly make true mischief with us, such as we do with the lower creatures... Do we then truly have a complete understanding of whether there is a family of creatures in the airy regions that are neither good nor evil angels, nor the souls of the departed, rather hybrid beings different from us and them, half angel, half human?

Glarus, the backdrop for a first-rate staging of the main plot, full of magical intrigue, where underworlds and overworlds stirred, powerfully encroaching on the concerns of the living. Hybrid ghosts of various origins, snickering, making mischief between the Wiggis, Schilt, and Glärnisch.

Lower devils, servile demons, and poltergeists who come at the beck and call of a maid. The hierarchy of the visible world carries on; what other option is there, even in the invisible world?

And this powerful being now sits with her bread and water above the heads of the council.

This could become dangerous for the sixty upright men from Glarus and the surrounding valley.

A maid, a weak woman, certainly.

But behind her the corruptor lies in wait. She who, if the devil prodded her, would finish those sixty to a man, practicing her witchery on them, robbing them of their virility on a whim, or ensnaring them with desire…

Is Anna Göldin chained? A farmer from Linthal asks.

The sergeant nods.

And is then ordered by the chairman to strengthen their security measures.

What's the use? Freuler the weaponsmith asks. Such people can pass through closed doors. And if they have any impatiens with them, locks open up on their own.

That's idiotic, says Streiff the butcher.

The trial goes on, but the presence of the witch is tangible. It crackles in the air and thoughts are kindled, secret wishes. One man whispers to his neighbor that last night he dreamed of witches riding naked on oiled brooms. The other responds: Carnal intercourse with a witch increases virilty. Take Doctor Tschudi for example. His wife is expecting their eleventh child.

We may now begin with the amicable interviews, says Chairman Marti.

At this Judge Tschudi steps forward.

He requests that the council still *adhere to the primary objective of the examination.*

I know this sounds absurd. After all, I am the one who has urged the matter. But I want one more attempt made to heal my child. I have heard — and this from competent sources — that *those who have corrupted may make their victims whole again.* Therefore I politely request of you, gracious lords, *to ask Göldin as is befitting if she cannot bring the child back to her former health,* as the canton scribe wrote in the trial record.

That the sergeant is bringing her food in person and the surprising smell of wine from the pitcher bring Anna to stark alertness.

Has my innocence been proven, Blumer? Or will I be questioned?

The sergeant sets the pitcher of wine on the table and gestures dramatically.

Before moving on to interrogations, they examined the child again. She is in a pitiful state and can neither walk nor stand. Her misery, if you could see it, would strike you to the heart. He pauses, but Anna sits there silently. The council now asks you on behalf of Doctor Tschudi if you can help.

Anna stiffly responds: How should I be able to help the girl? I haven't hurt her.

...but the sergeant moved her in this, that she without a doubt brought the child to evil, and if she held back the truth, then she would be put into the hands of the executioner...

Anna has gotten up, stands in the half-darkness, breathing quickly and loudly.

The sergeant urges. If you comply with their request, your punishment is sure to be milder.

Anna sighs. And asks for a night to consider it.

Suddenly all thoughts standing still.

Up to here and no further.

Chased over hill, height, and peak, breathless, but with the feeling of security returning. Then a chasm opens.

The methods of her pursuers are ingenious.

Bear traps covered with brushwood; pits, steel traps.

In spite of the approaching night, she can see clearly. She notes the edges of the pit, surveys it, and gazes into the depths through its cover of brushwood.

She can hear her pursuers panting behind her.

No step forward, none back.

If she refuses, they will call for the executioner.

If she assents, they will triumph: She has corrupted the child, therefore she can heal her.

Like a mouse to bacon she was driven to Glarnerland after years of scarcity.

Twice, three times she came back.

And now she is caught in the trap.

8

She wouldn't have survived those terrible years in Sax if she had not felt that there were still things ahead that she hardly dared dream of: rich cities, valleys with rivers of gold, Pennsylvania.

After she fled she had accompanied Katharina on her visits to births and sickbeds; in Werdenberg Castle the governor's wife had taken Anna to be Katharina's assistant. Anna can help me until she finds a new job, said the midwife, but around here the lords' homes are few and far between. At that the governor's wife said: In Glarnerland, where I come from, there are plenty of rich people. Anna should go to a relative of mine, the wife of Pastor Zwicki in Mollis. Her husband is ill, and their children are not all grown up yet. She is looking for a capable maid.

The Zwicki house: five stories, almost like a castle, with a watchtower where everything could be overseen: who is heading into the valley, who is heading out. And inside, just what a maid might dream of — bowls for a varied repertoire of dishes, silver cutlery, damask tablecloths. An oasis in the desperate times of the early seventies, when everyone had to buy grain from Egypt, carried on shoulders through Bellinzona and Chiavenna over the mountain passes. The poor ate meadow grass. Frau Zwicki handed out alms from the back door.

A charitable employer. She never needed to show the household's money twice. What will it be today, Maiden Anna? Of the best? A little more? They whirled over to the counter, currying favor with her. The maid basked in the glow of her employers.

Enjoy a hearty share in both the prosperity and ill fortune of one's employers, Anna, Frau Zwicki had said on the first day. Care for their welfare, honor, peace, safety, and health more than anything else. She was quoting from Lavater's *Morals for Servants*. Share in the status of the honorable family. Belong to them, even if it is only with the perspective from within the kitchen.

Then why does Anna eat in the kitchen? Dorothee asked.

Frau Zwicki's cheeks tightened, a touch of pink suffused her round face framed with wavy white hair. God-given distinctions, child. Anyone who tries to blur the lines is acting against the natural order. Stop order, and it will stop you. Anyone who would suspend it will fall.

When Anna first saw the young man who came home during his semester recess, she tripped over his brother Balz's tin soldiers. With a red face she kept herself from falling by holding onto the tiled stove inscribed with: Johann Heinrich Zwicki, God bless you.

So there he was. She knew him from his letters, which were of such delicacy, that Frau Zwicki could have them read to her during mealtimes.

"Frau Mama may give attention to her health, and not go out for too long, take the antispasmodic powder and the almond oil against catarrh…"

Dorothee read the passage a second time, and her Frau Mama dabbed her eyes with a laced handkerchief. Melchior painted scenes of the student life in Göttingen, focusing on what would interest his mama and leaving out what did not fit that mold.

"…went to Buchholz for a *déjeuner champêtre*, which is so in fashion now, since people have begun to read Rousseau and Gessner. The ladies with their wide-brimmed, yellow straw hats were like shepherdesses, and a little table was set up on the grass and spread with tasty things that Frau Administrator Fellinger's maids brought along in a basket. I sat there so comfortably; I watched the springing lambs and brooks and of course recognized everything as a superb *désguisement*, and thought with vivid longing of home, where it keeps pace with Rousseau in intimacy and the simplicity of the country folk…"

He could have been a poet if he were not studying to be a doctor, Dorothee said.

Anna served him at the table. He was different from his siblings: shy, of slighter stature. She felt his dark, lively eyes rest on her as she sliced bread for the younger children. You should still be wearing your scarf and reading on the lee side of the wall. After all, it's only April, Frau Zwicki advised and reminded him about his chronic bronchitis and delicate health. Melchior's eyes wandered beyond the edge of his book as Anna reached up under the laundry line in the orchard. Fluttering clouds hung in the föhn sky drawn through with blue streaks. When she brought out a tub of wet laundry, he jumped up and took her load from her.

Oh, no, you need not…

She fended him off, blushing.

Was she frightened by him seeing her as a human, a woman, and not a second class being? In Göttingen he had become interested in the aims of the English revolution and the ideas of the dissatisfied French.

He set down the tub. From above the pear tree through the open window, Dorothee could be heard playing the spinet.

Southerly wind, caught in the walled-in square. Trembling whorls of light, linen cloths billowing, Anna's bonnet taking wings that reach upward.

A ray of sun fell on her left eye, their gazes met. Chaotic fluttering to whatever goal, under a windy erratic sky that ripped open blue holes and shut them again with milky clouds.

A window was pushed open and Frau Zwicki called for her son. His father was suffering from another episode of heart trouble. The föhn wind threw everything that was thought to be stable out of balance. Melchior's book remained lying open on the wall and Anna read the marked lines as she went by:

…So much simplicity with so much understanding — so mild, and yet so resolute — a mind so placid, and a life so active…

This book was recently published, he explained to her later. The author: Goethe. He read her face while he told her the plot. His expressive, soulful eyes. The full-lipped yet disciplined cut of his mouth. The harmony and restraint expressed within that oval.

He pulled her into conversation and admired her way of freely answering, of calmly bringing up her thoughts, and her nimble, cheerful soul.

In an upsurge of comfort he slipped the book to her, against propriety. She read it all night, only slowly making sense of the letters since she was out of practice. From time to time the letters became blurry through her tears.

The pastor's wife found out about it because of the spent candles and reprimanded Melchior. The book of a free thinker — she knew it to be so through hearsay — is not proper even for a lady of standing to read, not to mention a maid. She should read Lavater, if anything.

She gave Anna one of his books of prayers and Psalms.

Anna did not like Lavater's Psalms; they were too cluttered with words, wedged into the straitjacket of meter. Psalms in their traditional form, with which she learned to read, were dear to her, a mighty river that pulled her along: *I will love thee, O Lord, my strength. The Lord is my rock, and my fortress, and my deliverer; my God, my strength, in whom I will trust...*

What she learned by heart in her youth had become her flesh and blood, an emergency reserve to draw from on a night like this.

The comfort of religion.

She had felt it for the first time as a sixteen-year-old in confirmation class in Meyenfeldt.

Finally allowed to sit down in a circle with others her age. It was a blessing for one who otherwise had to toil in house and stable from morning to night.

The pastor spoke of heavenly Jerusalem. Anna hung on his lips. Edification, comfort — *Jesus Christ, hear my languor. Hear me, friend of my soul. Shouldst thou give ear to a heart that weeps after your soul? —*

mixed with an earthly desire, for there were eyes gazing over from the boys' side, where the window opened onto a courtyard full of chestnut trees. The girls pretended not to notice and exchanged pictures with messages and paper lace: *For Anna, a keepsake for my dearest friend.* O, such righteous resolutions and intentions! Life was simpler, more transparent up until then.

9

On the morning of the 11th of March the officer is gone to the prisoner, to learn from her what she thought now regarding the business, ... to which Anna responded, they should bring the child in God's name. She would help her with God's aid and the assistance of the Holy Spirit; at which she sighed and moaned: O what an unhappy person I am.

What day is it today, Blumer?

March eleventh.

Today the child turns nine years old. One year ago I baked her a cake and put eight candles on top.

In the early morning she had lit a fire in the hearth with numb fingers.

Suddenly a shriek.

Anna Migeli was standing in the doorway in her nightgown and barefoot. Anna, you're on fire!

The child stared at Anna's hair, which blazed with the reflection of the flames. Anna's eyes glowed like a cat's as it prepared to leap on its prey.

Anna saw the girl trembling and went to her. She felt her pulse.

Were you afraid?

The child nodded. Your hair was full of flames! It could set the house on fire. And then the föhn will blow the shingles away and the wine press would burn, and so would the church and the watch house…

You silly girl.

Anna stroked the child's head until she calmed down. She looked up at the maid, who now seemed to have grown larger with the poker in her hand. Anna, whom flames obeyed.

When dealing with the devil, the camerarius says, one had best use a polite, ceremonial tone. The eleventh of March is a Friday, the child's birthday, and the council has decided that the *corrupted daughter of said Herr Doctor Tschudi* should be brought to the town hall at nightfall.

The shutters must be closed, Sergeant, and the doors barred. No candles are lit in the chandelier, which is shaped as Lady Justice with a fish tail. A single light is set on the floor.

The Herr Examiners and the lords of the *Ehren Commission* raise their hands to swear the pledge of secrecy.

Sizzling expectation.

The captain brings in the child, holding her in his arms, his head maternally inclined, lines of worry creasing his forehead, his ears sticking out. What devotion. He sits in the middle of the council chamber with the girl on his lap.

Now only the witch is absent, but they can hear her approaching steps and the clanking of chains.

Anna looks terrible, nothing at all like a witch; a deception they easily see through. She is still a stately figure of a woman. It must be a pleasure to search for the witch's mark on her, the mark the devil placed on her in some hidden place as a seal of his conquest. The executioner will do that. But it has not come to that yet.

Judge Tschudi steps forward and officially asks Anna to help the child. The request of a counterspell. Do you need herbs, medicines for it? (One certainly knows that people of her sort use herbs. Even Homer spoke of the magical herb moly, which Helen gave to Telemachus in his wine; St. John's wort routs the devil, fern seeds make whomever possesses them invisible, peony seeds take fear from children, not to mention mandrakes, those roots that resemble people and grow under the gallows from the urine of hanged thieves...)

I need nothing, Anna says. I will rely on my hands and prayer.

The lords of the *Ehren Commission* exchange meaningful looks.

But Anna does not notice. She sees only the child, her pale face with the fluttering look, the distorted leg pressed up to her body. Her words are recorded by the scribe:

You dear child, I thought your insides were suffering, I did not know your little leg hung like that, and more.

Gratified, they note the compassion in her voice and the expression on her face. They tell her: We will have mercy on you if you heal the injured child.

Anna Göldin felt the left unhealthy leg, held it up, and grasped it, pressing it back and forth, accompanied by several spirited sighs...

The candle on the floor gives Anna a demonic appearance. Hanging over the captain's head is Lady Justice with her mermaid smile. People swear oaths under this dubious feminine form of all things. The shadows of the *Ehren Commission* separate from their casters and climb up the walls: bent heads and limbs like spider legs on the ceiling.

...Herr Captain said that as the child's guardian, he was aware that the leg was stretching, and of some true life moving within, where it previously had been rigid and immovable, even during the fits of convulsions...

The healing attempt lasts two hours. Anna's face streams with sweat over the injured leg; her hands refuse any assistance. The lords of the *Ehren Commission* note in wonder: The child is as still as a lamb. She lets herself be tended by Anna, whereas only days previous she had cried out with every touch and kicked with her healthy leg during Doctor Marti's examination for the *visum et reperatum*. Anna is put back in her chains as eleven o'clock approaches and led to her cell.

On the evenings of the 12th and 14th of March the healing attempts are repeated in the town hall.

The sergeant reports that *the leg is a bit longer and straighter,* but the child still cannot walk or stand. I would like to try once more, but in the place where the evil began, in the Tschudi kitchen, Anna suggests.

Tuesday, March 15th, at eleven o'clock at night she is led from the town hall under the trees to the Tschudi house, *with all caution as ordered so that she might not escape.* The sergeant to her left. The captain to her right. One runner ahead and one behind her. Never before has such a dangerous criminal been led through Glarus, and the moon is rising among the clouds over the Schwammhöhe, casting shimmering light on the gravel path of the Tschudi garden while the scent of cinnamon from the yews wafts over. Through the back door into the kitchen.

Anna requests that no one be present except for the captain and Sergeant Blumer. *At which Göldin took all of the chairs there and put them in front of the table in the kitchen, with these words: This was truly an unhappy hour, when you and I were at odds.*

Anna pulls the child's stockings off. The wretchedly distorted leg, the contracted foot. She wants to heal the child, putting everything within her into this night.

Come in God's name, Anna Migeli, if I must be a witch to these people, I still wish to help you and do you no ill...

Anna goes at it with greater intensity. The sergeant reports later that it seemed to him as if the leg grew under the pressing, turning and grasping. She pulls it along its length, ... *in doing so, a loud popping and cracking sound came from the leg, almost as loud as when fir wood burns...* The listeners at the door hear the popping and rush in. The child is set down on the ground. She is able to stand alone and walk when led by the hand.

The members of the *Ehren Commission*, the girl's parents, the sergeant, and the captain are astounded by Anna's "arts." Shouldn't you go up to the chamber with the child, to put everything to rights? The captain urges. The child says she was given the treat there.

Then let us go up in God's name, Anna says. She leaves the reenactment to the captain. Sit on the bed in the chamber again and put your hands on her. For the sake of completion, shouldn't someone else be here?

Anna knows nothing of this.

The child declares, on the urging of the captain, *Ruodeli Steinmüller was there, too…*

To which Anna responds: *That is all just a flight of fancy.*

Anna is exhausted and soaked in sweat after the session. Doctor Tschudi and the *Ehren Commission* suffer her presence a while longer in the parlor, where something for her to drink is placed on the table next to her.

They were astounded by Anna's arts, Cousin Private Tutor and Apothecary. The child was ill for eighteen weeks; her father, who is known to be stingy, gave away half his fortune trying to heal her, calling for Marti, Irmiger… and in the end here comes Anna and the child is healed.

Has it helped Anna's situation?

No. People believe she is a witch.

Anyone who has unusual abilities must be getting it from the Evil One.

The devil comes in handy to them.

But they believe the child.

She only has to open her mouth and spit out words instead of pins. It just gushes from her: lies, rotten filth.

Words from the captain trickling into her ear. Words pumped in by that slit-eared, big-eared reed blower, who is the one starting all the lies, coupling the bad and the good. Hand-rubber, saliva-licker. If only he had stayed at his watch house window, the meddler. Vulture, nourishing himself on tears, sighs, and the moans of Tschudis. Irmiger made him believe there was a secret code on his behind that would only be revealed at the end of the world.

Is the child completely healthy now?

She still has stomach pains. The sergeant makes another request to Anna on Doctor Tschudi's behalf.

No end to the new hurdles and complicated assignments.

Like the seven-part tests in fairy tales. A spiral from which one must break free.

Tell the Herr Doctor to prepare the ingredients for a laxative. I will brew the draught myself and give it to Anna Migeli.

On the bed in the maid's chamber? Why not?

A yellow seed comes out in her stool. A nail seed that Doctor Marti inspects thoroughly and finds to be nothing more than a *saburra intestinorum*.

10

Hanging in the web of their questions, struggling to free herself, becoming hopelessly enmeshed.

On the 21st of March the first amicable interview.

It begins as harmless chatting, information about her: I am forty-four or forty-five (figuring the difference between 34 and 82 is not everyone's forte, especially since the school systems in both Sennwald and Glarus did not include arithmetic in their curricula before the revolution). Her home was on the Crüzgasse in Sennwald, her father was Adrian, her mother was Rosina Büeler.

No, I did not put any pins in the milk, not with my hands at least.

The inquisitors look at each other.

In the event that the subject denies it, they have prepared an interrogation from a reliable *General and Special Instruction* booklet from Bayern, which draws from the *Malleus Maleficarum,* especially from the section devoted to the lawyers: a criminal code outlining the types of execution.

The questions are already spinning in circles.

She cannot say anything to account for the pins. I've got to assume the Evil Spirit made me do it. She looks at the window. Swaths of mist range along the Glärnisch and gather on its outcroppings.

The Evil Spirit, Anna.

Heiz's lips protrude, his eyes glare wolfishly. Anna fears that her story was not enough to satisfy the lords. Better to turn back immediately.

She pauses for thought, which goes on the record.

Then she says with a sigh: In God's name, I put the pins in the milk.

Rain drums on the window panes. Governor Altmann, still hale though in his sixties, unfolds a large handkerchief and blows his nose.

The first interrogation lasts four hours, until late into the night. The second one the next morning is only superficially connected to the questions of the previous day. The questions leap straight from the needles in the milk to the one hundred and seven pins in the treat.

Are you aware of having given these things to the child?

Yes, I am aware.

When and how?

On that same Carnival Sunday, when the Frau Doctor went to the Lieutenant Bekker's.

Where?

Up in the maid's chamber in the Herr Doctor's house, as the child said, while I sat on the bed.

How?

In a treat.

Where did you get it?

Kubli notes in the record that here Anna is at a loss. This goes on; for over an hour she refuses to answer. Heiz stands at the window with his back to the subject, Kubli sits at his desk and sharpens his goosequill. Anna stands stubbornly and stares at the shadows gathering under the furniture.

They can smell her fearful sweat. Heiz wrenches open the window. It is raining in sheets and earthy scents waft into the interrogation room. Hovering over all of Glarus is the cool of moss, the damp of the grave.

The earth, softened by days of rain, slurps and gurgles and pulls all living things into itself until it is overgrown with moss. The earth has good digestion; it has ingested so much already, generations of mortals without a whimper, but their survivors take no offence. As they daintily run barefoot into the ravenous earth, such unawareness must make their hearts shudder within their bodies…

So, Anna?

If you do not answer, we will have to call the executioner.

She sighs and says: Steinmüller gave me the treat.

At this Heiz responds: *I note that you continue to sit as if frozen:* do *you wrong Steinmüller with your statement?*

Anna responds that she does not *know what* she *does.*

They read her testimony aloud once more. Then she states that she must retract her testimony: Steinmüller did not give me the treat. I got it from the devil. They eagerly seize on her statement.

In what form did he come to you?

In an terrible form.

Her face is bathed in sweat. She collapses and is taken back to her cell.

A few days of peace until the next interrogation.

At the end of March the cliffs of the Glärnisch are lit in the sunlight of the lengthening days; the shadows remove to the deeps and take on a violet hue, reminiscent of liverwort, which people pick at this time of year from among last year's leaves on the edge of the forest in Ennetbühls.

Melchior wrote of the mountains in almost ever letter that came from Göttingen. A silhouette fell out of one letter onto the floor. Anna quickly bent down, looked at Melchior's profile, then handed the picture to Frau Zwicki.

I am pulled from my books to the mountains whenever I read Haller's splendid poetry. I plan to go mountain climbing when my exams are finally done.

Any more of the roast veal, Frau Pastor? Anna balanced the silver platter.

Frau Zwicki waved her away: Later.

Mountain climbing is good for physical exercise and the refreshment of the soul: what delight, what bliss for a receptive mind to gaze in wonder upon the immeasurable mass of mountain…

He writes beautifully. Dorothee took a pause in the middle of reading. I believe he is quoting something, Frau Mama said.

Gessner, if I am not mistaken.

Everything in Melchior's letters sounds as if it could have been written in a book, Anna thought admiringly.

His mountain-roaming came to an abrupt end in only the second week of vacation; Frau Pastor asserted that Melchior's pneumonia came from bathing in the icy water of the Klöntalersee.

Around the same time the pastor collapsed one morning. As they were laying him in his grave, Melchior lay in his room with a high fever, wavering between life and death.

Frau Zwicki, exhausted by her nightly vigils, had an attack of nerves.

Anna took over Melchior's care.

Days when everything went wrong. The sick man's face became gaunt, his body decrepit. He lay there in the chamber lit with the light of July without complaint, silent, as if something solemn were occurring with the waning of his strength. She wondered whether there were ill patients addicted to playing this game of fading away. Her mother had been addicted to weakness. The doctor had little hope.

During the days of greatest danger, Anna did not leave his bedside. The window was wide open, but the July air was oppressive, an unmoving column over the square of orchard. The hollyhocks stood shadowless, without the usual hum of insects. The light faded into a white wall between the mountains. It was blinding. Something supernatural moved within these days.

Anna made sure that no birds came to the window ledge. If one were allowed to sit there, the sick young man would be dead by morning. The worst of it passed.

Anna took Melchior's hand hanging limply off of the bed and bathed it in tears.

Days, weeks of life returning. The trees and bushes in the garden regained their shadows.

When she brought him his food one evening, he drew her to him.

She pulled away and stepped back.

Why? He asked. A touch of displeasure in his face. She remained silent. She could not put her feelings into words. He, on the other hand, was a master of words. He said things such as: Love does not ask after differences imposed by a society whose boundaries are scorned by the great thinkers. It is doomed to collapse, Anna.

Or: When I think of those affected, ill-tempered daughters of standing, their moods, and their speech sprinkled with bits of French!

As the days went by, it became clearer to him that he desired her. What did it matter that she was a little older than him?

Something silent within her was at rest, growing.

Members of the Court of Five and of the Court of Nine, judges of the Morals Court, honorable lords of the three councils! So many bird catchers, but where are the birds? Here is a rare specimen finally caught in your net, a true witch who has fluttered into a corner of Glarnerland. The judges surround her, they watch her fidget and become more tangled in the mesh. So-ho! Off on the witch hunt.

Dorothea is having dreams that they will lock me up, Cousin Private Tutor and Apothecary. She is sleeping poorly. I'd like to make her a tisane from six ounces of sweet syrup, three ounces of Melissa water, and one ounce of cream of tartar. She won't go near the grating, the iron bars in my workshop. She is upset that Anna said all that nonsense about the treat and pulled me into the affair as the alleged confectioner.

I knew Anna would come back to reason, yes, she took everything back, Cousin, thank the Lord. It is not only the hare that ducks and weaves out of fear. No, they do not dare imprison me because of my considerable and prestigious kindred. A Steinmüller is no runaway maid, after all. Even the chief magistrate says that Pastor Jakob Steinmüller in Matt could have been a minister, a general, a learned man like Haller in the world outside. He's a genius with language yet remains humble. And then the Steinmüller dynasty of teachers in Glarus, of which you, cousin, are the fifth member and the focal point…

The apothecary laughs.

Beams of sunlight weave through the room, the measuring scale flashes. Then the door swings open with a powerful thrust.

In the name of the law.

Locksmith and apothecary stare at the runner in official colors.

By order of the noble lords of Glarus I am to bring you *ab instante* to the town hall.

Surely this is a mistake. Anna has taken it all back.

The runner, a tall man with a pimply chin and a periwig tied at the back by a ribbon, shakes his head.

During this morning's interrogation Göldin renewed all of her accusations against your person. This business must be investigated by the high authorities.

But Dorothea…

The assurance that he had first looked for the locksmith in Abläsch.

Go, Cousin, the apothecary tells him. You are a citizen with a good reputation. A hearing will secure your innocence. Otherwise the Steinmüller kin will come to your aid, even if it's not with such a blustering performance as the Tschudis made…

The first time the runner represented the power of the authorities without Blumer, his superior, present, it was a satisfying demonstration. But now he is annoyed by the locksmith who follows the summons with short, fidgety steps on crooked legs. He is forced to slow the purposeful stride that makes such an impression on the girls so as to match the little man's pace. This puny old man stinking of garlic, whom he must lead through the streets of Glarus to face justice! Only dogs and maids turn to look. Hardly coincidence that on the morning of the 29th of March, Doctor Tschudi is paying a visit to the town hall, *with his daughter, whose faculties were completely restored, to the righteous amazement of their most merciful lords, and who walked the entire length of the council chambers with neither discomfort nor distress nor assistance.*

Steinmüller witnesses the end of the performance. The child in a red velvet dress and a head full of curls set by their maid with a hot iron. She curtsies before the chair of the Protestant council and blows a kiss to the noble lords.

Here and there tears of emotion glisten on their rustic faces.

Oh, my soul. She walks. Without anyone helping her.

The child owes her regained health to the vigorous intervention of justice, Tschudi explains. The blessing of courageous action. Seldom does one experience it in such intense form.

Anna is not the subject of talk.

But the real action is yet to come.

Tschudi bends over his little daughter and asks her to find the man in the hall who gave her the treat on Carnival Sunday.

The silence of a tightrope act at the circus.

The bright eyes of the child, her glance wanders through the rows, leaving a trail.

Now her glance comes to rest on Steinmüller, who stands in the doorway between the runner and sergeant.

The girl walks to him through the parting crowd. Her dancing movements, her bobbing red skirt.

This man here.

As Steinmüller is led away, Tschuid explains that his daughter has never seen the locksmith before, according to his wife.

Is that possible in such a small town? Shocked murmurs, questions, objections.

11

Sudden fear, hollowing one out until only a thin façade remains of what one once was.

The questions of the examiners are mercilessly elaborate, snares set in interrogation methods borrowed from the *Malleus Maleficarum*, taking certain details for granted with the mandated questions of *Where* and *When*.

She pauses, catching a scent, searching for the answers to the questions presented by the inquisitors, the answers they have already determined.

Pursued, she ducks and weaves.

She blames Steinmüller. Then the devil. Then Steinmüller again.

She insists on this testimony, even though Steinmüller, locked up in the cell next to hers, resolutely maintains during two harsh interrogations on March 30th and 31st that he knows nothing of this business and has not been to the Tschudi house for a year and a day. On that terrible Carnival Sunday when this event supposedly occurred, he first went to church, then spent the day at home.

Anna, are you willing to confirm these statements under torture?

I am willing.

The amicable interviews are replaced with the territion. On April 4th, Volmar the executioner arrives from Wil. *He was instructed properly and respectfully before the commission.* The commission allows the nineteen-year-old son of the executioner, *who would watch and learn how the business proceeds,* to be present at the interrogations.

There are methods to terror.

This master of the subject knows the protocols: gradually increase the intimidation, first verbally, then physically. At the first territion the executioner appears in the corridor. Anna sees the compact man holding a sword. During the questioning he stands next to her, silent.

For the second territion, on April 5th, Anna is led down to the torture chamber. There she is forced to sit on the torture chair. As he shows her the various instruments, the executioner leans down so his face is very close to hers: it is wide, with deep grooves, not dark, merely withdrawn and serious. The lines around his mouth and nostrils speak to his precision; he could have been a bookkeeper in a compting house.

He shows her the thumbscrews or *polletra*; the ropes or *fidiculae*; the throat band with spikes pointing toward the inside; the torture stone; the tongs; the ladder rack, which is used to lift up the malefactor. To demonstrate, he binds the ropes around Anna's wrists. She feels it down to the marrow of her bones. Tears roll down her cheeks.

The passionless style of the master from Wil is renowned, as is the precise manner in which he carries out his duties.

Only the nineteen-year-old disrupts the session with his curious, lively eyes, never standing long in one place but pacing up and down and staring out the window.

Do you still claim that Steinmüller made the treat for you?

She nods.

On his urgent request, Steinmüller is led into the torture chamber.

His appearance incites greater agitation in Anna than the executioner did. He stands there, small and bow-legged, between the examiners. He appeals to the old Anna still hiding within her, scared and huddled in fear:

You should be kinder and not hurt an old man who never did you any harm. You know better than anyone that I am innocent.

His beseeching look.

Anna, they are playing us against one another, you must break the rules of their game. They sense that we know more. In our fearful perspiration they catch the scent of how different we are. We have never belonged to them, we sit straddling the fence, with one leg among them and the other in the shadow of the forest, among the mushroom gills, the white-winged ants, and in the chalices of flowers, from which secrets emerge at night.

Anna recants. Please forgive me, Steinmüller!

He reaches for her hand and thanks her through his tears, promising to pray for her.

After Steinmüller is led away, the interrogation continues with the exhausted subject.

They want to know how she corrupted the child without Steinmüller's participation.

Anna sighs and is silent.

Finally she goes back to the Evil Spirit.

The lords' inquisitiveness is insatiable when it comes to the devil.

Who gave you the items?

In the Evil Spirit's claw was a paper that said, there now you have it. I had desired such two days previous, and the Devil came to me twice, in a terrible, foul form...

Where, when, and with what words did you call the Devil?

I saw no one more from the kitchen window at 12 o'clock in the evening, and I called out, O Evil Spirit come and bring me something for the child, there is strife between us...

I did not see how the Evil Spirit came inside, he can get through any small opening.

After the third territion Anna must confirm her statement under torture.

Her naked body is pulled up the ladder, though again without any weights attached. She *gave a fierce, dreadful wail, but no tears were to be perceived.*

While she hangs there, tortured, they question her.

The same questions, always the same, like lashes with a whip. She keeps to her version about the devil. The devil gave her *red and yellow wormseed and white poison* wrapped in paper, and she put the ingredients in moist bread and gave it to the child.

This sounds plausible to the examiners but they determine it to be false since Anna Maria Tschudi knows nothing of bread, rather insisting on the treat prepared by Steinmüller.

On the 13th of April the second session of interrogation under torture.

Anna is lifted up with a heavy stone hanging from her bound feet. To the astonishment of the commission, Anna gives hardly a sign of pain, which is at first attributed to the devil, but the record notes: *The executioner from Wyl, however, who appears to be a very reasonable man altogether from his conduct, indicated that it is quite natural for her to find it less painful, for with the first lifting a stretching occurs in the limbs and in the second lifting the stretching no longer occurs.*

More questions while she is tortured naked. They say to her that the child knows nothing of the moist bread. Then she recants her statement about the devil and returns to the version about Steinmüller and the treat.

She has had enough. She is at the end of her strength.

On May 8th, the harshest torture, in which *the offending woman was stretched with the heavy stone for the second time, left to hang a long time and jerked roughly during the main questions, yes, altogether pained to the greatest..."*

The scribe cannot bear to hear any more of her moaning. He is haunted by it at night. His hands, clammy with sweat, reach for a new sheet. The innocent paper sympathizes with him, that he has to contaminate himself with this intricate line of questioning. What sort of horrid business is this that he must write down, proceedings he must set his name under, so complicated that it cannot be redeemed by lovely calligraphy?

Do you confirm your statement now, under torture, that Steinmüller gave you the treat?

As she is tortured with glowing tongs, Anna squeezes out a moan and a faint *yes.*

The executioner's son vomits.

Kubli ends the record: *Finally Göldin is released, wan and harshly battered, and taken back to the new tower.*

Anna and her abused body.

She dreams during the night of a star approaching. All of the previous Annas leap out of it like shooting stars. As if her soul wished to say, you are not only the current one, you are still the other Anna's.

As she dreams, Melchior is in all of her thoughts.

Anna, lie with me, you will make me well.

... and the health of the masters; you must care for their wellbeing more than anything else...

You are a cornucopia, a delicious fruit, I want you.

... even when they are ill you must wait upon them with willing patience, and see to all right business at their beck and call...

He gazes a long time at her body.

Anna, where do you begin, where do I end?

Usually he says nothing more. She likes that.

When he speaks, his phrases and words sound to her as if they were taken from books, as if another were speaking through him. She stands on the bank, parted from him by his stream of words. She feels closer to the silent Melchior.

... she found work. A young man of reputable family, worthy of a better fate, fell into her snare, and was the victim of her evilly organized passions... (Lehmann)

He himself had noted that she was pregnant. Not a word passed through her lips. He comforted her. All this will pass. Christmastime softens everyone's hearts, even my mother's.

Anna, a bowl in her hands, stood in the doorway to the dining room and gazed at the tree decorated with candles. The lights trembled as though they were reflected in water.

Come, Anna. According to family tradition, on Christmas Eve the servants sit at the table with us, mindful that it was in the stable that our Lord…

Anna grew weak sitting behind the golden-edged plate. The child, a scion of the Zwickis, was there with her at the table and stirred in the maid's belly.

They moved over to the parlor to give out the presents.

The younger children engrossed themselves in their games.

Melchior and his mother sat on one of the carved benches the house's builder had mounted in the window bays, conversing agreeably, the playful discussion a harmonious conclusion to the evening.

Anna, Frau Mama.

The eyes of the Frau Pastor Zwicki had no lashes. Her lids were nictating membranes like those of birds, twitching at the slightest irritation.

Her grace, her knack for serving, her agile, untarnished spirit…

Frau Zwicki's brows, naturally placed high and arching, indicated a condition of continuous shock.

Of whom do you speak, Melchior?

Of Anna, Frau Mama.

The nervous, bird-like twitching of her head.

A Zwicki may not have a *mésalliance*, Melchior.

Times are changing, Mama.

Causerie, mon cher, from the plush chairs in the salons. None of our aristocratic sons may decline the branch upon which he sits. Our family honor, Melchior.

Family honor is everything to you, Camerarius, says the young Private Tutor Steinmüller. It is obvious in the list of works you have composed. Your fondness for your radiant house is not just found in your genealogical tables and trees of the "distinguished, renowned, and ancient noble family Tschudi of Glarus," but in your historical works you also extol your compatriot and relative Ägidius Tschudi regarding taxes, and in the *History of the Canton Glarus in Biographies of the Distinguished Men of the Tschudi Family*, the significant men form the family tree, branches and twigs. The historical events merely form the foliage, blossoms, and ornamental leafwork of the Tschudi tree.

I, a Steinmüller, fear that Anna will add a dark leaf to the history of the Tschudi family, if you, Camerarius, indisputably a man of vast scholarship and unusual income, do not bring the business to an acceptable turn. It still lies within your grasp to…

The camerarius indignantly gasps for breath.

Then this object of so much gossip presently playing out in Glarus has been spread outside the land and presented in such a distortion! And as a result, the head of the Protestant church in Zurich, Antistes Ulrich, has sent him this letter, dated the 19th of April.

Allow me, most Magnificent Herr, to inquire with you regarding some business that interests me greatly. Is there truth to the rumor that there are people in Glarus who claim, in all earnestness that a certain maid put a large number of needles and iron nails in the usual food of a young child, along with who knows what else?

Is it true, too, that men of rank and prestige where you live have been taken in by these ridiculous ideas? Is it true that the unfortunate person who is the subject of these laughable suspicions remains imprisoned and is even in danger of losing her life by the hand of the executioner for this imaginary crime?

No, I cannot, I will not believe this by the honor of your church and your free state. It would be indeed much too sorrowful, if one in our enlightened century wished to reinstate those horrible tragedies that dishonor humanity as much as Christianity, which have been performed here and there under the protection of superstition, in a Protestant land and, to be sure, in one where noble Freedom has most excellently made her home. This would not only amount to the greatest shame of your own most praiseworthy state, but also of the united confederation and especially, too, of our reformed church before all of enlightened Europe. Most Magnificent Herr, I speak not only my own opinion, rather that of all reasoning men in our city, from the smallest to the largest. And I consider myself bound by my conscience to reveal this to you in brotherly trust…

I will only add the assurance that I wish you farewell with the highest respect.

Zurich, the 19th of April 1782
Joh. Rud. Ulrich, Antistes

The camerarius immediately sits down at his desk. He expresses his warmest gratitude for the letter and gives a long-winded explanation of the story of the illness with reference to his own diary. He then answers the antistes' question of whether it is true that men of rank and prestige have been taken in by these ridiculous ideas, in the following way:

It is a clearly improved situation. All the corrupting materials previously mentioned were evacuated from the child, though accompanied by incredible pain. This can be attested to and confirmed under oath by a large number of reasonable, honest witnesses who observed everything closely, though they watched with sorrow. The corpus delicti was found, not only apparently, but substantively. The snake that bit the innocent child made her healthy again. The miserably abused child has been cured and transformed. How can this now be a ridiculous thing to believe? To believe what one sees with one's own eyes and hears with one's own ears? In the enlightened current century will we not only use our sound senses but also be allowed to trust them?

...

But supposing that they take Göldin's life, what right has the neutral public to place blame? Are those unhappy ones who corrupt their own bodies' fruit and miserably mangle the innocent children of their good masters, are they not deserving of punishment — yea, of death?

...

Grant me your worthy friendship, and remain assured always of my utmost respect.
Glaris, the 14/25 April 1782
Joh. Jacob Tschudi, Pastor

The second attempt on New Year's Eve.
Melchior with his mother on the window bench.

The light of the snow on the Wiggis reflected on her white hair, a net holding it in place so that no unruly locks could force their way through the mesh.

Me and Anna, Frau Mama.

Yes?

Anna is expecting a child.

I'm going to be sick, Melchior. My smelling bottle!

12

Those who visit the valleys of Glarus wander through a large bustling factory. These poor shepherds, concealed between frightful cliffs, exposed to every rockslide, have managed to master numerous branches of trade simply by their spirited activity and endurance and present an outstanding example of a most industrial people. (Johann Gottfried Ebel, 1802)

The world is rolling, continually advancing toward perfection as designed by God, in which the snake loses its poisonous bite, the weed is destroyed, the wild growth is pruned back, and the factory chimneys of the cotton printers, the cotton spinners, and the muslin weavers tower over the grand houses of Glarus: signs of activity and ambition, refined nature advancing through civilization, a clean, neat world.

But as always, thinks the camerarius, a woman threatens our terrestrial Paradise and brings the best of all possible worlds out of balance.

From the pulpit he looks down at the people below, separated by gender down the middle aisle, on one side the dark mass of married men, in heavy coats of brown cloth smelling of dirt and stable, of the fruitful kingdom of Earth upon which he might scatter his seeds of words.

The women across the way a lighter hue, inconsistent with the jumble of bonnets, dresses, and here and there some fashionable French garb. A steady unrest passes like a breeze through their rows, possibly because of the long-stemmed flowers they hold in their hands; they move them now and then, smell them during the sermon, or lower them into their laps in boredom.

Women, he thinks, cannot be reached. In spite of their refined ways, even Solomon called the woman a sea — unformed, simple material.

Up until now, the locksmith has responded to the trick questions with barbed defiance and pulled his head out of many snares with a glib answer, giving back questions full of natural wit. The thought of his relatives' assistance gives him strength. The sergeant's maid smuggled a copy of a letter into his cell, a letter from the Steinmüller kin to the authorities. His fate had mobilized the intelligentsia of the family. The brilliant writing style indicates that one of the two Jakob Steinmüllers, either the young private tutor or the learned pastor in Matt must be the author, or so one of the examiners said. The locksmith is deeply moved by it. The pastor, who was a field minister in the Sardinian-Piedmontese batallion, had galvanized the Glarus authorities once before with a letter, urging the "Herr Landlords of Glarus" to adopt more democratic policies after an uproar broke out in the rural community. Now he wrote to ask how it could be possible for a man who had the magic arts of Hell at his disposal to have worked as a locksmith for sixty years, leading an honest life, never attracting attention, and not once benefiting from his magical arts?

In spite of the letter, Steinmüller remains imprisoned and during a territion the executioner threatens him with torture if he does not reveal the truth.

Steinmüller responds that the authorities will be responsible if his old body no longer works after the torture.

Then a second letter is passed to him, which his wife had dictated to a fourteen-year-old girl:

Dear Husband, may God strengthen and comfort you in your sorrow and mercifully help to redeem your innocence. But regret your naivety, that you could deal with that cursed whore, so irresponsibly handsome and deservedly suspicious, that you invited in a monster with a dog such as her. This is the crime for which you sit imprisoned.

She gives him precise instructions on how to behave in order to be released.

On May third, Steinmüller demands to be brought to see Anna again. In the presence of the examiners, he calls her a hellhound and a whore, and takes off one of his shoes and throws it at her. They ask him what is meant by his behavior. He says: I have lost my patience; my circumstances have only worsened with civility, pleading, and praying. My imprisonment was made harsher and my food was withheld. Finally he has to admit that his wife wrote to him.

Now they torture him more vigorously, especially after they search his home and workshop and find a book, "in which there was writ all manner of secret tricks for the corruption of people."

Before the torture he is advised to confer with his relatives. But the authors of the letter are not allowed in. Instead two other relatives loyal to the authorities are admitted: Treasurer Zweifel and the old Schoolmaster Steinmüller. Neither give him any help and instead press him with threats: If you continue to deny it and later confess under torture, then we will never again accept you and yours.

The interrogation immediately follows the discussion, in the presence of his relatives.

Steinmüller, exhausted and harassed, avoids the gaze of the examiners and the devoted teacher.

Through the windows there is Glarus, an eschatological Glarus, violet in the shadow of the mountain.

In a vision he sees the captain sitting at the top of the Glärnisch, with Anna Maria Tschudi in his lap, half child, half old woman clothed in a snowy garment and with roaming eyes, in which a miniature Glarus stands reflected in disarray. The houses are charred, the streets are full of debris, and Doctor Marti sits at a table on the Adlerplatz, which is covered in rubble, writing a *visum et reperatum* and diagnosing an illness for which the world will perish, and Governor Altmann's rasping voice reverberates in the chaos of these end times:

Are you aware of having given Anna Maria Tschudi the treat?

I am.

When they ask him how he made it, he comes up with:

I took steel chips and a chunk from a stone that had long been lying by the butter market, summoned of David's stone. A young man brought such stones from

Kleintal, they are believed to house gold; I still have some of the stone at home; when such a stone is broken, a golden kernel is revealed in the middle, like in actinolite; I also took yellow, burned vitriol, eggwhites with meal, a little charred plaster and honey, then made a dough and baked it on an iron plate in the smithy with charcoal fire.

We certainly need not adopt Papal nonsense, says the camerarius to Treasurer Zweifel on the way home. The *Malleus Maleficarum* should be left behind with its abstruse fantasies of incubi and succubi and people who can fly, take on the form of an animal, or ride on a broomstick.

But the fight against corrupters has its tradition in the Protestant church as well, even the Antistes in Zurich must know that. Calvin preached this in Geneva regarding the woman of Endor, that "the Bible teaches us that there are witches and that they must be slain." In 1545 Calvin decisively intervened in the witch trial of Peney. And finally even Luther himself struggled with the devil according to a few statements, and four witches were burned at the stake in his Wittenberg.

I maintain that witchery is a sin of pride more than anything else, in which one aims to go beyond the limits that God has set for men. I consider women especially prone to this sort of pride. As reprehensible and antiquated as the *Malleus Maleficarum* may be in certain places, it also contains good points to start from. Its authors, Sprenger and Institoris, traced the word "femina" from "fe" and "minus:" "fe" meaning "belief," and "minus" meaning "less." Women doubt and deny belief more quickly, which is the groundwork for witchery.

A woman is a wild garden that must be tamed and cultivated. The jurist and political philosopher Jean Bodin described the dominance of man over woman in this sense. The dominance of the intellect over nature, reason over desire, and soul over body.

13

Anna, your love is too absolute.

This sun's eye above us fills the entire sky. I'm afraid it will singe us.

Reason, Anna. No fool's paradise.

It would go against reason to force this.

I will give you the address of a colleague of mine at the maternity hospital in Strasbourg.

To exit through the only hole in the fish trap, away from Mollis toward the Kerenzerberg mountain.

To depart from something she loved. The air cooled with every step taking her further away. In the higher altitudes it began to snow but the streets remained the color of a wet slate. On and on, into the temperate zones of mediocrity, where passion no longer intersected with the plans of ambition.

Anna, it is still not the right time for love, there is no room for it. It would be choked off.

Let me give you money, Anna.

She declined his help. And decided to find a position as a maid in Strasbourg and put the child in foster care, even if it meant that she must give every guilder she earned to his foster mother.

Adieu, Anna.

Until later. A new time is coming.

Even my Frau Mama will not live forever.

Not hearing. Single-mindedly moving on, no looking back to a scene that shrank and warped forever. Leaving a piece of oneself behind like a lizard in flight. The time of our dreams is old before it is born, set on the tile with the Greek idyll.

Away from Ziegelbruck on a bateau toward the Zürichsee, the Rhine, and Strausbourg; can the baby grow in this cold penetrating her clothing? Even the moon hanging over the mountains of Glarnerland as they slowly retreated behind her was green — an unripe fruit.

Snow colored the Linth valleys white under a sky of milky glass.

The relentless trickle of snow, of bits of time, floating past frosty reeded banks, beyond place and time.

The feeling of time trickling away in prison, too, of slipping away from the here and now. To what end?

Only the mountains remain and will always remain, unmoving even when she, Anna, still exists only in Kubli's strange records. The mountains are eternal but the human is short-lived, fluttering and delicate with his defenseless, vulnerable body.

Visum of Medic. Doct. and Morals Court Judge Joh. Marti. On the order of that sage church council I betook myself with the Ehren Commission to the cell of the unfortunate Steinmüller, where the executioner revealed the dead body, with a cord around the throat, to all the highly honored lords present, and after removing the cord from the throat, he displayed the deeply etched blue ring, full of blood, the sight of which, along with the foam from the nose and mouth, clearly revealed the true cause of this unfortunate death, strangulation by the cord, as it thus appears to the highly esteemed and merciful lords' most obedient and loyal servant, according to his duty. (Joh. Marti)

The locksmith chose to put his trust in the iron bars, whose reliability he knew from daily contact, and not in his relatives; on May 12th he hanged himself on the bars of the door in his cell with a strip of sheet. Steinmüller has escaped forever with his secrets and his hellish recipes; the members of the council, which is quickly convened, feel cheated. Nothing but proper that the criminal should still be punished, even in death, according to the record:

The noble lords require, by their oath yet in mercy, that his body, as that of a poisoner, shall be given over to the executioner, closed up in a sack by the same, bound fast and put outside on a rope through the uppermost window, carried away on a cart, and taken to the gallows on the Reichsstrasse, there the right hand will be hewn off, and the body buried three feet deep under the gallows, and finally his right hand shall be nailed to the gallows — so that he will have his well-earned punishment and serve as a terrifying warning to others.

Steinmüller's estate is confiscated by the Protestant treasury.

The descending sun has colored the cliffs red; now twilight lies as a gray filter on the leaves of the linden trees.

Even in dream the gray twilight casts its shadow on the green meadows. The houses, themselves as massive as the Zwicki house, shrink into a flat backdrop that easily folds up on itself, compliantly clustering together. Melchior, as he slowly walks through the orchard with book in hand, disappears through the east door. Anna remains behind under the twilit trees.

Trees. I feel so close to you.

The wind rushing between the cliffs has taken the last of the leaves.

Should they put Anna behind bars for life, or hand her over to the executioner? Long discussions unfold in the council. There are people who desire to prevent a death sentence at all cost, and at their request the city of Zurich has proposed to take possession of the "witch of Glarus" and sentence her to hard labor.

That troublesome word *witch*. It must be stricken from the record and avoided in her sentencing, Kubli. Corrupter, poisoner, evildoer, monster: anything is less embarrassing for us.

To Zurich? That's all we need, the Tschudi camp says. The letter from Antistes Ulrich clearly demonstrates the arrogance of those people who consider themselves enlightened. They will cast doubt on everything, turn the light in a new direction, put devil's horns on us instead of on Anna, and dub us backwoods idiots…

Anna must go. As certain as death.

The entire horrific episode must be buried fathomlessly deep under the gallows.

You are not absolved of whatever happened between you and Anna, says Frau Tschudi.

You shouldn't get excited in your condition, says the judge. I'll banish all the rumors from the world.

15

The Zwicki house in winter. It shoves off from the snowdrifts like an ark, the central glimmering light is Melchior's reading lamp on the table next to the stove with the blue mountains and entire paradises on its tiles.

Winter trees, fluttering with birds, and clouds caught in their skeletons.

The moment of truth has arrived.

Anna's feverish body, once in full bloom, now martyred, is dragged before the council because Tschudi demands it.

The *corpus delicti*, supported by the sergeant, in the center of the council chambers.

Judge Doctor Tschudi stands at an appropriate distance from her. He asks her to reveal, in front of the sixty upstanding men of the council, whether she had carnal intercourse with him or if he ever demanded anything indecent of her.

The furtive expressions on the councilmen's faces. They have warned Judge Tschudi. It would be a mistake to put this question to Anna publicly. Now, when she has lost almost everything, she could exact vengeance on him with a lie at the last minute.

The slightest hint of equivocation from her mouth will condemn him to eternal ridicule.

And above Anna hangs that secretive, smiling chandelier woman who is half fish, half Lady Justice.

The council chairman, Major Marti, sticks out his voluminous lower lip as he always does in tense moments.

But Anna sees only her former employer.

He is uncertain. She can read the Herr Doctor's expression.

His doggish whine, his blinking, begging eyes under heavy lids.

This is how he had looked at her from the doorway as she washed herself, half-naked in the kitchen. How their eyes had met back then. How his eyes had slid away, searching for a less incriminating path. Anna had forced him to look away. She watches as the man's form shrivels, becoming black and small, a crow with fluffed up feathers on a tree in the Zwicki garden in winter. She hears her own voice through thick snow drifts: he was always appropriate.

Trees in winter subsist on the vertical line, each alone, in proud growth. And the farmers in her hometown walk this way over the wintering fields, dropping shadows in the glare, every man for himself.

Thank you. You may take her away, Sergeant.

Anything else, Judge Tschudi?

Chairman Marti twitches his hand, as if to chase off a fly.

Yes. I will not pay for the cost of the trial. You must get the funds elsewhere. The delay and increase in cost occurred because the defendant was warned.

But the final trump card is still in Tschudi's hand. His face changes imperceptibly; the malicious smile does not suit him, the chummy nod of the head.

I have learned a few things from a trustworthy source.

The fine Herr Zwicki of Mollis did not warn Anna on account of his Frau Mama, rather to keep secret certain calamities… Acts of the flesh never happened in Glarus, but they did in Mollis. That is where Anna did in fact once leave with a large belly, and gave birth elsewhere. I recommend that the noble lords determine how to deal with this delicate situation...

Summer trees. Bits of shadow come together and form sinkholes. The scent of leaves. Their essential oils keep the mosquitoes away, Frau Zwicki had said, and hung a cluster of walnut leaves over Melchior's bed.

The air from the linden trees wafts in. A tangle of voices.

People have gathered on the Spielhof. Music pours into Anna's cell followed by the babble of words.

A poem by the camerarius is recited.

An adaptation to be sure, boldly translated from French, embellished to the utmost:

Ye noble linden trees!
Through your cool canopy streaming
Sunlight doth flare.
Delightful nymphs sojourn
Upon grounds such as these:
Ye oft reborn leaves,
Stalwart witnesses to our simple fathers.

Anna, in waves of pain, embalmed in the flowery fragrance. Brandy distillate pools in her pus-filled wounds that run down her ankles where the torture stone tore into her.

Heaven protect you from ruin
Delivered by time, wind and the axe.

Applause. The camerarius thanks his audience for their gracious attention.

No, I do not aspire to be a poet laureate. It is merely a whimsical break from the stresses of daily life. I leave dallying with muses to the residents of lovelier countrysides. We always must seriously contend with the mountains here…

Thoughts muted by constant pain.

Dreams surrounded by wounds.

She made no mention of her relationship to Melchior, though other maids would have boasted of this and her employer.

A secret one carries for a long time will sink continually deeper within oneself.

If the secret were taken away, it would destroy her innermost being, from the roots of the secret all the way to its most delicate branches.

The next morning Blumer brings her once more to the council chambers.

The inquisitors desire an answer in a delicate matter.

Do you admit to having become pregnant by Doctor Melchior Zwicki in Mollis?

Anna stares at Altmann's rosy hands folded over the swell of his belly.

Then she said, not without pride: I admit to it.

Where did you bear the child after leaving Glarnerland?

In Strasbourg.

Where is it now?

Dead.

She will say nothing more. She knits her brows and stares out the window. She fervently hopes they will spare her a personal confrontation with Melchior Zwicki.

But Zwicki has already been interviewed.

Kubli recorded his answer: He admits to it. But he hopes that the gracious lords will forgive him after such a long time (eight years) for this "oversight."

Her Melchior, ingrained in memory, is utterly distinct from the coward she encountered half a year earlier at the St. Gallus market in Glarus. She had roamed among the stands, finally stopping in front of the bonnets and tuckers from Venice and the Netherlands. She tried on a bonnet with frills and lace and looked for her reflection but the mirror was dark with people roaming the market on the Adlerplatz.

In one group, Melchior.

She turned with the bonnet still on. The wind played with the bonnet's frills.

She involuntarily took a few steps toward him. Their eyes met again after so many years.

Melchior faltered, his eyes uncertain, then walked past her as if he did not know her.

She stood numb, the bonnet had slid so it was lopsided on her head. She did not hear the vendor with his compliments: I'll give it to you for a lower price. For your lovely hair. Anna tore the bonnet from her head.

She walked on, dazed. She did not notice a coachman she knew from Mollis silently tiptoeing around her. When she stopped, he whispered to her: Doctor Zwicki will be waiting for you at six in the alder grove.

It was already getting dark as six o'clock approached. She turned onto the main street. A hunter with a dead chamois on his back was walking in front of her. With every step the chamois' head smacked against the rough fabric of his rucksack; its eyes were open.

Anna followed the hunter up to the butter market, where she turned around decidedly.

A half moon hung over the Wiggis as she walked home. The other half of it was still faintly visible, a pale blue echo.

It can be harder to find the sky here than in other lands. Upraised eyes and the head tilting back requires strength. Anna's neck is stiff, her eyes tired.

Let out my chains, Blumer.

I want to stand at the window. Air. I'm going to suffocate.

With eyes uplifted, she can still find a small bright patch between the mountain peaks: pure concentrated sky.

Anna, Blumer says, the council has decided your fate. The sentence is death by the sword.

That is, thirty votes were against and thirty-two were for your death. Kubli should have fought harder for you, and now he has to compose your death sentence.

The camerarius and Deacon Marti have been charged by the lords of the council to prepare you for a worthy death…

From the question booklet, adapted from the *Heidelberg Catechism:*

What are the levels and series of Christ's humiliation?

His poor birth and life; his suffering and death;
His burial and descent into Hell.
Prove this to me.

Philippians 2:7. But He made Himself of no reputation, and took upon himHimself the form of a servant, and was made in the likeness of men.

Question: Which is the other level or series of the humiliation of Christ?

His great and harsh suffering.

How did Christ suffer?

In body and soul.

Prove this to me.

Psalm 22:16-17. They pierced my hands and my feet.

I may tell all my bones.

Matthew 26:38. My soul is exceeding sorrowful, even unto death.

Question: To what end did Christ suffer?

So that He with his suffering might redeem our bodies and souls from eternal damnation, and procure for us God's grace, justice and eternal life.

Prove this to me.

John 3:14-15. And as Moses lifted up the serpent in the wilderness, even so must the Son of man be lifted up: That whosoever believeth in Him should not perish, but have eternal life.

Was it necessary that our redeemer die?

Answer: This is most certainly true."

Now the camerarius' verbose explanations of death, in which no one meets the midnight blackness of death. So Anna asks to be alone. The camerarius says they are ordered there by the authorities to uplift and comfort her. Then at least do those things in silence, please. Deacon Marti holds out the cross to her. She gazes at it silently and kisses it.

Outside the camerarius says to the deacon, Anna is clinging to Jesus as her last beloved. He sounds angry, as if something in his image of the world has gotten confused by this.

June 18th, 1782.

Glarus, agitated by witch fever. The chimneys of the cotton presses and the spinners' roofs stab an orange sky.

Their work set aside, the people of Glarus and the surrounding valley villages stream together. The sixty men of the council have arranged themselves on the Spielhof, the halberdiers' cockscombs and the sergeant's scarlet cloak wave in the breeze.

Ceremonial pageantry for Anna's death.

She is led out of the scriptorium of the town hall, where she was guarded by six halberdiers for the last two days.

Such light. After weeks of dim twilight, it stabs her eyes like a knife.

CRIMINAL TRIAL and VERDICT of ANNA GOELDIN from Sennwald, who has been sentenced to death by the sword:

The miserable evildoer presented here, who has been imprisoned for 17 weeks and 4 days, most of that time bound in irons and chains, called Anna Göldin from Sennwald, has confessed under amicable and painful interrogation, that on the Friday before the previous Carnival between three and four o'clock in the afternoon, she left Herr Doctor Tschudi's house and went at a quick pace behind houses and over streams to the locksmith Steinmüller, who of late killed himself in a most unfortunate way during his arrest by the authorities, to request from him that he give her something to harm the second oldest daughter of Herr Doctor and Judge Tschudi, Anna Maria, whom she felt evil toward, to make the child wretched with that infamous, despicably evil purpose…

This snake of words, winding and tangling in knots. Flicking its tongue, it lifts its head and finally bites itself in the tail… Kubli is reading too softly, the people behind him protest.

… observe the great breach of trust and wickedness this evildoer performed as a serving maid against her employer's innocent daughter, observe the indescribably horrid and outrageous illness that lasted almost 18 weeks long and the deplorable conditions previously described, which the little daughter suffered to general amazement… also observe her previous evil moral conduct, of which to be sure, she was castigated in her hometown by the hand of an executioner, as ordered by her rightful authority out of mercy, on account of giving birth in secret to a dishonored child and hiding it under the blankets…

Anna, these words, at the mercy of all these eyes.

… for which she is condemned by the gracious lords upon their honor: that this poor evildoer shall be delivered to the executioner as a poisoner for the punishment she deserves for her crime and to become an impressive example to others, and shall be led to the usual place of execution…

By order of the authorities, Anna is not to be led to the gallows through the fields already planted, but instead through the beech wood: if the criminal's shadow fell on the grain, the circle of evil would begin anew when it reached the bellies of the town folk in the form of bread.

Anna slowly trudges under the weight of her chains, leaning on Blumer's arm on the last hill and gasping for air, and the great bell begins to toll in the village. A crowd pressed close together is already there awaiting the spectacle. Bakers with baskets go through the rows. It is an old custom for bread to be given out to children and the poor during an execution.

... by the sword she shall be executed from life to death, and her body buried under the gallows, her assets confiscated...

Glarus in the light of June. The roofs, streets, and cliff walls shimmer. Anna in the midst of hazy white, deceit sweeps her away while the mountain masses crowd together, flanking and crushing all those yet living, and now only the rumble of stones and the cry of birds.

Afterword (Eveline Hasler)

The trial triggered unexpected publicity. In the *Reichspostreuter* of January 4th, 1783, the term *Justizmord* ("judicial murder"), was coined in connection with the witch trial. The historian August Ludwig Schlözer printed the same article in February 1783 in the Göttingen *Staatsanzeigen.*

Even before these publications, an essay had appeared in the political/satirical newspaper *Chronologen* in Nürnberg, which was so cynical that the authorities of Glarus summoned the publisher and writer trained in the style of Voltaire, Wilhelm Ludwig von Weckherlin, to Glarus to appcar before the court. Weckherlin did not appear, with the explanation that only "insanity would ensue if I were to appear before a court where the prosecutor is also one of the judges."

At that, Weckherlin's "impudent libel" was burned by Glarus's executioner and the author was declared an outlaw.

Heinrich Ludwig Lehmann, candidate for the Doctorate of Theology in Ulm, came to Glarnerland only after Anna's execution. He was able to get an idea of the course of the trial from conversations with witnesses. His *Letters to friends and acquaintances on the notorious, so-*

called witch-business in Glarus was meant as a defense for the authorities of Glarus.

Tellingly, there was no criticism to be heard of in Switzerland.

In Glarus the original texts disappeared right after the trial; copies of the originals were found in the estate of the examining magistrate Heiz in 1783 and 1818.

In connection with the case of Anna Göldin, there appears to have been a small epidemic of children who presented similar symptoms as the "bewitched" Anna Maria Tschudi. In 1783 *The Gazette de santé or Public Journal of Medicine* mentioned the case of convulsive seizures suffered by the nine-year-old daughter of Heinrich Egli and the case of a boy from Weisslingen who vomited nails, needles, and stones. The attempts of Irmiger from Pfaffhausen, described in detail in the medical periodical, were unsuccessful, and finally the boy admitted to a Canon Schinz that he had simulated the fits. Seven years after Anna's execution, fourteen-year-old Heinrich Kubli in Netstal, not far from Glarus, suffered from convulsions and visions. He spat up needles, nails, hooks, and, in a new variant, juniper berries. Once again an outsider was suspected of using magic, one Elsbeth Bösch from Toggenburg, and taken into custody. This time, influenced by the Zurich examples, the "corrupted" boy was isolated and observed at the manse. With good food and play, the phenomena soon disappeared, and the boy was allowed to return home healthy. The imprisoned Elsbeth Bösch, fearing that a similar fate to Göldin's awaited her, jumped from the window of the interrogation chamber and shattered her feet upon landing. She was acquitted but remained crippled for the rest of her life.

In spite of the high costs of the Göldin trial (the lords of the court were paid attendance fees of one doubloon, or 8 guilder and 15 kreuzer, and the executioners Vollmar, father and son, were paid 314 guilder) Doctor Tschudi was not required to pay any of his own money. Thanks to the liquidation of the Steinmüller assets and house as well as the monetary fine of Doctor Zwicki, the Protestant council accrued a net amount of 754 guilder. This included Anna's 16 doubloons.

Acknowledgements and Sources

Official documents of the Goeldi trial (transcripts by Schlittler and Heiz) extant in the *Glarus State Archive* (www.gl.ch).

Records Sax-Forsteck.

Baptismal register Protestant community of Sennwald.

Zürcher Gesangbuch. Zurich 1598.

Tissot, Samuel-Auguste. *Avis au people sur sa santé*. Lausanne 1761. German edition *Anleitung für das Landvolk in Absicht auf seine Gesundheit, Oder: Gemeinnütziges und sehr bewährtes Haus-Arzney-Buch*.

Lavater, Johann Caspar. *Gereimte Psalmen*. Zurich 1768.

Lavater, Johann Caspar. *Taschenbüchlein für Dienstboten*. Zurich: David Bürgkli, 1772.

Anon. "Avertissement." *Zürcher Zeitung* (9 Feb. 1782).

Wekhrlin, Wilhelm Ludwig. "Hexen-Process in Glarus." *Chronologen. Ein periodisches Werk*. Frankfurt and Leipzig: Fellseckerische Buchhandlung, 1782.

Schlözer, August Lienhard. "Abermaliger Justizmord in der Schweiz." *Stats-Anzeigen* (Göttingen)

2.VII (1782-83): 273-7.

Lehmann, Heinrich Ludewig. *Freundschaftliche und vertrauliche Briefe, den so genannten sehr berüchtigsten Hexenhandel zu Glarus betreffend.* Zurich: Johann Caspar Füessly, 1783.

Afsprung, Johann Michael. *Reise durch einige Cantone der Eidgenossenschaft. Neunter Brief.* Leipzig 1785.

Ebel, Johann Gottfried. *Schilderungen der Gebirgsvölker der Schweiz.* Vol. 2. Leipzig 1802.

Heer, Joachim. *Der Kriminalprozeß der Anna Göldi von Sennwald.* (Jahrbuch des Historischen Vereins.) Glarus 1865.

Gehrig, Jacob. *Das Glarnerland in den Reiseberichten des XVII.-XIX. Jahrhunderts.* (Jahrbuch des Historischen Vereins.) Glarus 1943.

Winteler, Jakob. *Der Anna-Göldi-Prozeß im Urteil der Zeitgenossen.* Glarus: Verlag Neue Glarner Zeitung, 1954.

Aebi, Richard. *Geschichte der evangelischen Kirchgemeinde Sennwald.* Buchs 1963.

Fischer-Hombuerger, Esther. *Krankeit Frau.* Bern: Hans Huber, 1979.

Historical Background: Anna Goeldi, the Trial, and its Reception
(Waltraud Maierhofer)

On June 13, 1782, Anna Goeldi, age 48, was decapitated in Glarus, Switzerland. According to eighteenth-century customs, middle and lower class women's last names were appended the syllable "-in" or an "-n" when the name ended in "-i." This is the historical form used by Eveline Hasler in her novel. The contemporary expression "the Goeldin [woman]" in today's language is Anna Goeldi and therefore used in the following.

The verdict said that Anna Goeldi she was found guilty of poisoning and causing a mysterious disease in a daughter of her former employer Doctor Johann Jakob Tschudi (1747 – 1800), who was a physician and held high offices in Glarus as a member of the cantonal council and judge. Anna Maria (called Annamiggli) was eight years old at the time. Rumor had it that Tschudi had had sexual relations with his maidservant, and it must have been part of the interrogation, but among the extant documents only that part can be found where – before a verdict was announced – he was released from the accusation of sexual relations with the maid.[1] Where does the accusation of witchcraft come in? The term is avoided in the death sentence, but it was central throughout the trial, in which torture was applied in order to get a confession to poisoning the child and to being assisted by the devil.

Switzerland at the time was not a democracy, but a feudal society; there were 13 sovereign territories, which were oligarchies (Hauser 151-53). The canton of Glarus was (as were Uri, Schwyz, Unterwalden, Zug, and Appenzell) one of the so-called country community democracies where the "Landsgemeinde" was the highest political authority; this outdoor-assembly of all citizens (which excluded women) gathered on a certain day each year and voted on its authorities, laws, and criminal cases. In spite of this assembly, Glarus, like other cantons, was ruled essentially by a small number of families. There were other areas which were serfdoms to the cantons or free cities. There was no separation of power. Jurisdiction was in the hands of the executive power, the Council, and the highest member of the administration ("Landammann") was also the highest judge. The councilors were in their office for life and had absolute power. Glarus had Catholic and Protestant citizens, and therefore had three councils, one for each denomination

---

[1] This introduction is much indebted to the following book by Swiss law historian Walter Hauser who researched additional documents related to the case of Anna Goeldi not known when Eveline Hasler conducted research for her novel: Walter Hauser, *Der Justizmord an Anna Göldi. Neue Recherchen zum letzten Hexenprozess in Europa.* 2nd. ed. (Zurich: Limmat, 2007), here 9. In the following, page numbers from this source are provided in brackets.

and the Common Council, which was in charge of important cases including such calling for the death sentence. Morals were strict, and in 1775 an office was reinstated which was in charge of improving morality. Since 1744 unwed mothers had to wear a red cap and women who became pregnant outside of marriage (this was believed possibly only by non-citizens of Glarus, had to stand in the pillory and were then banned from the canton for three years (Hauser 159-60). Witchcraft, including the "corrupting" or poisoning of children, had been eliminated in the Glarus criminal code of 1698. Only according to earlier editions of the code, persons found guilty of witchcraft were to be burned at the stake or buried alive (Hauser 102-103).

Law historian Walter Hauser has advocated that Anna Goeldi was the victim of a power struggle between two of the leading families in the canton of Glarus, the Tschudis in Glarus and the Zwickys in Mollis. A second victim was Rudolf Steinmueller, a 59-year-old married man, master metal worker, and citizen of Glarus. He had a reputation for making mysterious mixtures, experimenting, and reading forbidden books (Hauser 96).

Anna Goeldi was the daughter of a poor couple in the Sennwald near Zurich (Hauser 53). They were not serfs and her father worked as a knife grinder and sacristan (Hauser 53). At an early age, she had to earn her meager living as vagrant servant with various employers. She never married. According to the warrant description of 1782 she was "rotund and tall, her face without scars or other imperfections, with a rosy complexion, black hair and eyebrows, and grey ... eyes" (translated from Hauser 61). Fictional descriptions adapted the description of the warrant and visualized her as a beautiful, stately woman.

Another half sentence in the document referring to her eyes as unhealthy and mostly reddened may stem from the fact that she was already believed to have the "evil eye" (Hauser 173-75). As the warrant further described, she spoke dialect and was quite well-dressed, even fashionably, for her standing.

Her first child, which she bore in secret in 1765 during her time as a servant in the parsonage in Sennwald, died of suffocation during its first night (see Hauser 53). The father of the child had left and enrolled in the army. Without a trial, Goeldi was put in the pillory as a child murderess and condemned to six years house arrest (Hauser 54). However, she escaped and found employment in the canton of Glarus with none less than the highest politician, *Landammann* Cosmus Heer. From 1768 on, Goeldi was employed by the Zwickys in Mollis in the canton of Glarus. She had an affair with the son of the family Melchior and had to leave when she became pregnant. Supposedly, she gave birth to a son in Strasbourg in 1775 and gave the child away, but no evidence could be found (Hauser 54-55).

In September 1780 she was employed by Tschudi as a maidservant. A year later, there was supposedly a fight between servant and daughter, after which, on three separate days (October 19th, 20th, and 22nd), needle pins were found in Anna Maria's milk cup and bread at breakfast. Doctor Tschudi fired the maid, accusing her of putting the pins into the cup and endangering his child. Goeldi insisted on her innocence, but left their house and stayed with the metal smith Rudolf Steinmueller. He was a relative of the Zwickys and had married a distant relative of the Tschudis but he had no contact with the Tschudis (Hauser 95-99).

Still no signs of witchcraft – for our rational perceptions. What started the legal procedure was not the fact that Goeldi was formally denounced as a "witch" at this point as would have been required for a trial in earlier times. Rather, it was Goeldi herself who, upon Steinmueller's advice, went to the authorities to seek justice from her former employer in the form of her withheld wages, her belongings and savings which were still in the Tschudis' house. They were which considerable for a servant. The authorities in this case were the highest cantonal politician or *Landammann*, Johann Heinrich Tschudi, and the highest member of the clergy, the Protestant priest. The name of the latter was identical with that of her employer: Johann Jakob Tschudi (1722 – 1784). Both were closely related. The vicar Johann Jakob Tschudi was bestowed the office of Camerarius in the following year of 1782 and will therefore be referred to as such in the following in order to distinguish him from the physician Dr. Johann Jakob Tschudi. Both the *Landammann* and the Vicar dismissed the case and advised Anna Goeldi to apologize to her employer in order to get her belongings and then leave the canton. Goeldi followed the advice; she apologized on October 27th and in return got her clothes and savings which she deposited with Steinmueller. Nothing happened in legal terms – yet. Anna Goeldi left Glarus on October 29th and went to her relative, Catharina, in Sax in the Werdenberg district (today St. Gallen canton).

However, one month after Goeldi's layoff, in November of 1781, Anna Maria got sick. She had some form of mysterious seizures, called in the records "goutish seizures" (Hauser 8). Today she might be diagnosed as epileptic. Doctor Tschudi was unable to cure her. She was found throwing up pins and other sharp metal objects. This only occurred when her parents and/or the Vicar were present. The factuality of these findings and the natural possibility of this was never questioned, nor was it investigated whether Anna Maria would "vomit" any such objects when she was separated from her family. Now Doctor Tschudi accused Goeldi of having corrupted or bewitched the child, and no other explanations or attempts to cure her were sought. On November 26th the Evangelical Council sent a courier or "runner" to have Goeldi arrested.

Goeldi was warned about the order of arrest by another courier sent by Johann Melchior Zwicky. Steinmueller also sent her a warning but the letter was confiscated by Doctor Tschudi. Goeldi fled beyond St. Gall to Degersheim in the Toggenburg region, near Lake Constance. On December 4th, interrogations of Zwicky and Steinmueller began in Glarus. Several days later the Evangelical Council moved to pass the case on to the "Common Council" but the request was denied, stating that it was already in good hands and reports to the Common Council would be sufficient. On December 9th, Doctor Tschudi requested a public warrant of apprehension for the maid. It was issued on January 21, 1782 and printed in the *Zuercher Zeitung* on February 9th. He also requested that all members who were related to Zwicky recused themselves from the case (Hauser, 185).

A second medical opinion was sought. A medical attestation of Anna Maria was issued by Dr. Johannes Marti. Marti (1745 – 1819) was then the physician of highest renown in the canton of Glarus, not someone we would suspect of believing in witchcraft. He was the first to inoculate against cowpox, he researched the medicinal uses of sulfur springs and founded a spa in Linthal (Hauser 15, 80). Between December and the middle of February, interrogations continued with Doctor Tschudi and his wife Elsbeth, with Goeldi's cousin Catharina Goeldi and other witnesses. Goeldi was found, arrested, and brought to Glarus on February 21st, 1782. Apparently, the Protestant Coucil had to ask the Common Council for approval to proceed – which it did, although not in open terms. Doctor Tschudi insisted repeatedly that the case was to be judged solely by the Protestant Council (Hauser 68-75).

Doctor Tschudi was a fairly modern, well-trained and respected physician, as was Doctor Marti. Did they really believe in witchcraft, or did they have another agenda, purposefully deceiving everyone? About twenty witnesses who observed the expectorating were heard in the investigation, but the girl was never observed in isolation. She maintained a healthy appetite and sleep pattern. It appears the pins were always found by her mother, with Camerarius Tschudi also present (Hauser 74-5). It was believed that the pins had grown in the body from bewitched food. Today, we will find it incredible that the medical possibility of this was never questioned.

Recently Walter Hauser has convincingly argued that Tschudi needed to prevent that his affair with the maid from became public (see Hauser 65-68). Because of the strict moral standards of the time and region this would have cost him his office and public standing as judge and councilor, not to mention the all-important honor of the family— which is what did happen to the Zwickys during the course of the trial. Doktor Tschudi pushed for the trial to be led by the Protestant Council under the authority of his close relative Vicar/Camerarius

Tschudi who supported him for the same reasons. The Camerarius was also a family historian and wrote a ten-volume history of his ancient noble family (Hauser 154) whom he believed to be chosen by God for special honors.

If Doctor Tschudi did not question the possibility of sharp metal objects growing from poisoned/bewitched food, a belief found elsewhere in Switzerland at the time, then no one else would, not even the outside medical expert brought in for the trial. In addition, that expert was by no means neutral. Dr. Tschudi and Dr. Marti had studied together in Basel, they were both members of the judicial body for marriage and moral cases, not to mention friends (Hauser 78). Marti's first attestation had only to do with the discovery of the pins. It did not try to explain the pins in the body of the child. Instead he offered that only the person who had "poisoned" the child could also heal her, that person being the "monster maid herself" (document, translated from Hauser 79).

Why did Goeldi not bring up the affair with Tschudi? Or did she? At the time, trials in Switzerland were held in secret. The part that whitewashed Tschudi is extant, but the original trial transcripts "disappeared." This is one of the reasons why the case has been so fascinating for writers of fiction and historiography alike.

The examination began on March 9th and Dr. Johannes Marti gave a second attestation on Anna Maria, this time regarding her contorted leg and foot, a result of the seizures. He noted that her left foot was totally "useless, aching, and contracted against her body" (translated from Hauser 79). The attestation got even stranger. The "medical expert," and the council with him, argued that only the woman who had "ruined" or bewitched the child could heal it – a common superstition at the time. This was a no-win situation for the accused: If the child was healed, it would prove that she had caused the disease. If not, it would prove Goeldi's evil will (Hauser 8). Reluctantly Goeldi conceded, insisting on her innocence. After several attempts in March 1782, the leg straightened and relaxed under her hands and Anna Maria was able to walk again. A laxative, given by Goeldi, got rid of Anna Maria's stomach pains.

Predictably, this was not the end of the trial. On March 18th, Anna Maria told the examining committee that Goeldi had given her a sweet cookie or biscuit and that Rudolf Steinmueller was present at the time. Anna Maria hardly knew Steinmueller, and it is strange that she would name him. Hauser therefore considers it more likely that a member of the council, Balthasar Tschudi, suggested the answer in his questions, and the child simply repeated (Hauser 96)? This technique had been very common in witchcraft persecutions. Goeldi had to undergo three formal interrogations. In the third she stated that Steinmueller had given her the treat, and the metal work master was then also interrogated. The council insisted on a confession of witchcraft. A torturer and executioner was brought in. After three interrogations in the presence of the executioner, Goeldi revoked her accusation of Steinmueller, accusing instead the devil as the cause of the evil. According to the outdated legal procedures the accusation of witchcraft allowed three applications of torture. After the first one on April 11th, 1782 Goeldi "confessed" that the devil had helped her prepare the sweet treat (Hauser 8). Anna Maria was not interrogated. There was some back and forth in Goeldi's "confessions," as Anna Maria changed her accusations.

Goeldi retracted "confessions" made under torture. The child stated that Rudolf Steinmueller had made the treat, and Goeldi "confessed" to this version on April 13th. On May 6th and 7th, Steinmueller confessed having made the treat, but renounced later on the same day, then again confessed to having given it to the girl two days later. Before he could be asked to repeat his confession, he hung himself in prison on May 12th, 1782 (Hauser 8-9). He was informally buried on the execution site, with his right hand cut off and nailed to the gallows. There was one last interrogation on May 19th, during which Goeldi told details of her life and pleaded for mercy.

The fact that she showed few tears during torture was taken as proof that she had supernatural powers and was in league with the devil. It is not quite clear what part her earlier pregnancies and the fate of her children played in the interrogation. Possibly, the council tried to sentence her for infanticide because they found no proof in the Tschudi case.

Because Goeldi was a "foreigner" from Zurich, on May 24th, several members of the council asked the magistrate in Zurich to imprison the accused in Zurich in case she was not executed. Zurich agreed. The other councilors, however, did not agree with this solution, and they were physically attacked by citizens of Glarus (Hauser 149). There was even a petition which accused the council of judicial arbitrariness and demanded that criminal cases should be judged by the assembly of the citizens (Hauser 149). The demand was denied and the petitioner punished.

On May 31st, Doctor Tschudi insisted on an affirmation of the passages that freed him from the allegations that he had sexual relations with Goeldi. At the same time, her pregnancy by Zwicky became known to the Council. It was probably denounced by Doctor Tschudi, and Zwicky had to pay a penalty. On June 6, 1782, the Protestant Council came to a verdict: Goeldi was to be decapitated for poisoning. It was a tight vote with 32 voices for death, 30 against (Hauser 142). She was executed and buried under the gallows. Camerarius Tschudi delivered a sermon at the execution site about God's justice and punishment of sinners, invoking God's mercy for the "guilty woman who had fallen so deeply" (translated from Hauser 8).

The council confiscated the estate of Steinmueller and his widow. In addition, the widow was required to pay a penalty for the letter she had written to her husband in prison. Zwicky also had to pay another penalty for warning Goeldi. The city of Glarus had a total monetary gain of 754 guilders from the trial. Today, this sum would amount to several thousand Swiss Francs (Hauser 142-43, 183). Because of his adultery, Zwicky was prohibited from all political offices, and as a result the Zwicky's were no longer among the most powerful families. Doctor Tschudi's honor remained untainted.

Several more cases of "bewitched" children spitting pins and needles or having seizures occurred in the following years in Switzerland. However, these children all were soon brought to admit that they had simulated the condition (see Hauser 75-6) and/or they were "cured" when placed under observation. In 1789, again in the canton of Glarus, a 14-year-old boy spit up nails and other objects and had seizures. Again, an outsider, a woman from Toggenburg, Elsbeth Boesch, was accused of witchcraft. In this case the authorities observed the boy, found that he was simulating his afflictions, and charged the parents with fraud (Hauser 76). Boesch was acquitted, but in the mean time had already jumped out of a window for fear of torture and broken both feet. She remained crippled.

Johann Melchior Kubli (1750 – 1835), the councilor who recorded the Anna Goeldi trial, became a senator of the Helvetic Republic during the Napoleonic era and an opponent of the death penalty (Hauser 42-3). Cosmos Heer, former *Landammann* and Goeldi's former employer, left politics (Hauser 44). Almost all members of the Tschudi family who were involved in the trial, died soon thereafter: Elsbeth in 1789, after giving birth to three more children who all died within a week; *Landammann* Johann Heinrich in 1783, Camerarius Tschudi in 1784 and his two sons in 1782 and 1784 (Hauser 173-75). Dr. Tschudi lived until 1800. He took part in the failed rebellion against the French in 1799 and was incarcerated. Anna Maria, the "bewitched" girl, married a merchant in 1794, and they emigrated to Ukraine, where she died giving birth to her eleventh child in 1810. Nothing else is known about her husband and surviving children (Hauser 174). The rest of the Tschudis' offspring were not very fortunate either, writes Hauser, and the last known grandchild of Dr. Tschudi died as a drunkard in New York in 1851 (Hauser 175).

Criticism of the trial was silenced and censored in Switzerland but published in newspapers, legal journals, and books in Germany, Denmark, and Holland. Glarus officials were criticized and ridiculed for believing in witchcraft and accused of abusing their power. In two 1783 articles in German newpapers, a historian and professor of political science, August Ludwig von Schloezer, coined the term "judicial murder" with regard to the Goeldi case: an innocent person had been murdered, "wilfully and even with all the pomp of holy justice" by the agents of jurisdiction (translated from Hauser 146). Journalists as well as historians and law historians have since investigated the documents and facts, though they were at first obstructed by resistance from the officials in Glarus, and then by the fact that the trial records "disappeared" (Hauser 26-27). Only parts were found in a copy three decades later in the estate of one of the examining judges, Jost Heiz, and given to an archive (Hauser 27).

Glarus could not stop the advance of Enlightenment. More and more citizens criticized the ruling families and authorities and their abuse of power, demanding to be allowed to participate in political decisions. Anna Goeldi was not the only case in which jurisdiction was abused by the ruling families in their struggle for power, but it became the most well known case. In 1798 Napoleon conquered the Helvetic confederation, and the old elite had to cede their lands. The serfdoms became independent. Napoleon reformed jurisdiction, abolished torture, and took other steps towards a liberal and democratic constitutional state.

Today, Anna Goeldi is remembered not only in fiction, although the popularity of Eveline Hasler's novel may even have influenced local politics and sparked historical research and legal efforts to rehabilitate her. In 2007, in the town of Glarus, Switzerland, the Anna-Goeldi-foundation was formed. According to its Web page (*Anna-Goeldin-Stiftung, Glarus.* Www.Annagoeldin.ch) it supports not only the memory of one particular woman, but aims to help members of minorities, marginalized groups and victims of arbitrary judicial decisions. Mollis, another town in the canton of Glarus, dedicated its town museum, the Zwicky-Haus, to the memory of Anna Goeldi (*Orts- und Anna-Goeldi-Museum Mollis*. Annagoeldin.ch). In 2007, the 225th anniversary of her execution, Fritz Schiesser, as representative for Glarus in the Swiss parliament, called for Anna Goeldi's exoneration. In September 2007, the Swiss parliament decided to acknowledge Anna Goeldi's case as a miscarriage of justice—news which made it even to *BBC World News* and to *Youtube*.[2] Finally in August 2008, the cantonal administration of Glarus followed suit and officially rehabilitated Goeldi.[3] She is remembered with special events every June. In 2012, Zurich tourism inaugurated special city tours following the last days of her freedom, "Anna Goeldi: The Last Witch of Switzerland" (Zurich.com).

---

[2] Imogen Foulkes, "Europe's Last Witch-hunt," *BBC News, Switzerland*. News.bbc.co.uk, 19 Sept. 2007. Web. "Europe's Last Witch," *Russia Today,* November 15, 2007. Youtube. Web. A detailed list of news coverage with links is on "Pressespiegel" of the Web page of the Anna-Goeldi foundation, Annagoeldin.ch.

[3] See coverage in the news see for example "'Last witch in Europe' cleared," *Swissinfo online*. Swissinfo.ch. 27 Aug. 2008. Web.

About the Novel

Eveline Hasler's novel *Anna Goeldi: Last Witch* with its simple yet literary style became a bestseller. It was not the first fictional book about Anna Goeldi, though. Hasler's novel appeared in 1982, the bicentenary of Goeldi's execution. It was the heydays of the women's movement, and equal rights for women were a hot topic. In Switzerland, it was only in 1971 that women were granted suffrage on the federal level and in 1981 equal rights for men and women became part of the federal constitution. Individual cantons were still slower to institute such measures, and the last one was forced by federal law in 1990 to let women participate in politics. In that sense it is a feminist work.

Hasler's "careful" approach puts a lot of weight on historical documents. They are identified by italics, explained in the context, and referenced at the end of the book. Hasler lets the documents speak for themselves without providing further extensive background information and explanations. It is not a continuous and chronological narrative that pretends to know what "really happened." Nor does the author present a full-fledged fiction with vivid dialogue and detailed, romanticizing descriptions. There is no bodice-ripping love scene, although the author opens the doors to several scenarios with the father of Goeldi's first child, with the young Zwicky, and with Tschudi. Nor does she draw on the horror and goose-bump effects of torture scenes. Possibilities are presented as such. Yet, in the sparing dialogues and reflections, Goeldi appears as a fairly independent-minded, strong, and self-assured woman with a strong sexuality, a pioneer of women's emancipation, a feature that this work shares with other fictional works about persecuted women. There is no narrative "I" except in the short first chapter which describes Anna's home region as stony and links her last name to it, stemming from the word for bedload, till, or rubble, which becomes a recurring motive in the novel. The author definitely advocates for the outsider and the rightless. *Anna Goeldi* is a very engaged and engaging examination of a historical character and case of injustice.

Waltraud Maierhofer, The University of Iowa

www.ingramcontent.com/pod-product-compliance
Lightning Source LLC
Chambersburg PA
CBHW070431120726
47910CB00003B/735